"If you really want what's best for Teddy, please don't rule yourself out. You might make a better father than you realize."

James knew the only reason he didn't discount the suggestion immediately was because of that gentle touch on his forearm. The cool brush of Lydia's skin along his. It made it impossible to think about anything else but her. His heart slugged hard against his ribs. His gaze dipped to her lips as they parted ever so slightly.

An invitation?

Or wishful imagining?

If she was closer, he would kiss her. He couldn't decide if it was a good thing or a bad thing that there was a vacant seat between them, keeping them apart. Instead, he covered her hand with his, watching her all the while.

Her pupils widened a fraction. Even in the dim light of the kitchen, he could see that hint of reaction. A sign of shared desire.

She didn't pull away.

* * *

The Rancher's Bargain by Joanne Rock is part of the Texas Cattleman's Club: Bachelor Auction series.

Dear Reader,

One of many fun things about writing a Texas Cattleman's Club story is revisiting Royal, Texas, and having the chance to work with the other authors who are setting stories there. So often, writing a book is a very solo endeavor. Most of the time, a book is imagined by the author and written and researched by the same author. But with the Texas Cattleman's Club, the writing experience is more communal. Research involves fun exchanges with other authors in the line.

It provides a great chance to compare notes on what we're doing, catch up with friends or get to know authors I haven't worked with before. This time out, it was a special treat to visit more with Reese Ryan and Joss Wood in particular since their stories fall next to mine. Seeing how these talented ladies create their characters and how they construct their story worlds inspired me. And I hope it shows in the special care we give to Royal, Texas, and the people who live and fall in love there!

Happy reading,

Joanne Rock

JOANNE ROCK

THE RANCHER'S BARGAIN

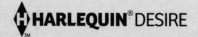

HARLEQUIN® DESIRE

Special thanks and acknowledgment are given
to Joanne Rock for her contribution to the Texas
Cattleman's Club: Bachelor Auction miniseries.

ISBN-13: 978-1-335-60337-1

Recycling programs
for this product may
not exist in your area.

The Rancher's Bargain

Copyright © 2018 by Harlequin Books S.A.

Printed in U.S.A.

www.Harlequin.com

Joanne Rock credits her decision to write romance after a book she picked up during a flight delay engrossed her so thoroughly that she didn't mind at all when her flight was delayed two more times. Giving her readers the chance to escape into another world has motivated her to write over eighty books for a variety of Harlequin series.

Books by Joanne Rock

Harlequin Desire

The McNeill Magnates

The Magnate's Mail-Order Bride
The Magnate's Marriage Merger
His Accidental Heir
Little Secrets: His Pregnant Secretary
Claiming His Secret Heir
For the Sake of His Heir
The Forbidden Brother
Wild Wyoming Nights
One Night Scandal

Texas Cattleman's Club: Bachelor Auction

The Rancher's Bargain

Visit her Author Profile page at Harlequin.com, or joannerock.com, for more titles.

One

It is okay to say no to unnecessary crazy.

Lydia Walker repeated it like a mantra while she read the digital headline from a story that had run in the Royal, Texas, newspaper earlier in the week while she'd been out of town.

Local woman boosts charity bachelor auction with $100K bid!

Seated at her tiny kitchen table with a cup of coffee grown cold, Lydia hovered her finger over the scroll button on her cell phone. She wished she could just swipe right and not worry about the "local woman" who happened to be her irresponsible sister Gail. The impulsive sibling who did *not* have $100,000 to her name. What had Gail been thinking?

In spite of herself, Lydia started reading the article again.

Gail Walker, a local entrepreneur, made the surprise bid on Lloyd Richardson, a local rancher. Ms. Walker could not be reached for comment while she is out of town on a romantic getaway with her chosen bachelor, but the Great Bachelor Auction master of ceremonies, James Harris, said he's grateful for the generous donation that benefits the Pancreatic Cancer Research Foundation. "This is what the event is all about..."

Closing her eyes, Lydia flipped the phone facedown on the table to stop herself from going over the story a third time.

Definitely unnecessary crazy.

She had just gotten back into town after a visit to her mother's home in Arkansas for Thanksgiving, a trip she'd been guilted into since she hadn't been home in almost two years. Her mom had used the time to corner Lydia about being in Fiona's upcoming wedding to a fourth husband, making the holiday a total disaster. Lydia had wanted her sister to make the long drive with her, but Gail had insisted she needed to stay in Royal and personally oversee her fledgling grocery delivery service. An excuse Lydia had accepted, proud of Gail for doing something fiscally responsible for a change.

Ha! Apparently, Gail just wanted to stay in town to bid on a sexy bachelor during the event at the swanky Texas Cattleman's Club. Had the word already gotten out around town that Gail didn't have the money? Lydia scanned the Royal paper for more news but found only stories about the auction's lone bachelorette, Tessa Noble, and her date with a local rancher. There was no follow-up article about Gail's date or her outrageous bid.

Yet.

Lydia's stomach knotted. How could Gail do something like that to a *charity*, for crying out loud? Furthermore, they shared the same last name. How did it look for the Walker women, both trying to start their own business, when they didn't pay their debts?

Anger flaring, she flipped her phone screen toward her again and dialed her sister's number. As the oldest of eight siblings, Lydia was used to high drama in the family. But for most of her life, the main perpetrator had been her mother, a woman who had parlayed her parenting experience into a successful homemaking blog, *House Rules*. Fiona Walker's online followers loved her "whimsical" approach to childrearing that Lydia viewed as flighty at best and, at times, downright dangerous. Lydia had hoped Royal, Texas, would be a fresh start for her and Gail once the youngest of their siblings was old enough to fend for himself with their mom.

But now, with the mortifying news of Gail's over-the-top bachelor auction bid, Lydia had to admit that her sister hadn't fallen far from the maternal tree.

"Lydia!" Her sister squealed her name as she answered her phone. "You'll never guess where I am!"

Frustration simmered.

"I certainly hope you're at the Pancreatic Cancer Research Foundation explaining how you're going to magically make one hundred thousand dollars appear," Lydia snapped, powerless to restrain herself. "Gail, what on earth are you doing?"

Anxious and irate, she paced around her half-finished kitchen in the house she'd been slowly renovating to one day open an in-home child care business. She nearly tripped on the flooring samples she'd carefully laid out by the sliding glass door leading to the backyard. The toe of her slipper sent Spanish cedar and mahogany samples flying over the ash and buckthorn pieces.

"I am having a romantic holiday with the man of my dreams," her sister retorted, her tone shifting from excited to petulant. "Is it too much to ask for you to be happy for me? For once?"

Lydia covered her eyes with one hand, remembering her mother had said those same words to her—almost verbatim—just last week when Lydia refused to be in her wedding. Now, her head throbbed while the morning sunlight poured in through the back door. "I'm happy that you're having a good time. But I'm very worried about how you're going to cover the bid you placed at the bachelor auction. Have you spoken with the cancer foundation?"

"I'll bet that's why my credit card didn't work yesterday at the spa," Gail mused. In the background, music that sounded like it came from a mariachi band was growing louder. "I forgot about the payment to the bachelor auction."

"What payment?" Lydia pressed, heading back to the kitchen table to clear her plate and cup. "You don't have the kind of money you bid."

She held the phone on her shoulder, pinning it to her cheek while she set the dishes in the sink.

"And I'll figure it out after vacation, okay, Ms. Worrywart?" Her sister raised her voice to be heard over the music. "Oh, and just FYI, I'm ignoring calls from anyone I don't know this week."

"Who has been calling you?" Apprehension spiked. "The charity people?"

"No, the guy who was in charge that night. John? James?" Gail sighed. "Just forget it, okay? Right now, I've got to get back to my margarita before the ice melts!"

"Gail, wait—"

But her screen already read, "Call Ended." And she knew her sister well. There wasn't a chance Gail would answer if she phoned again.

It is okay to say no to unnecessary crazy.

The words had helped Lydia survive her teenage years. But right now, the mantra didn't roll off the tongue so well when she thought about how the local folks who had worked hard to raise money for charity were being misled. The Texas Cattleman's Club had hosted the event, and their members were a who's who list of the town's most influential people. Lydia wanted to put roots down in Royal. She'd already bought the fixer-upper property to start her child care business here. The last thing she needed was a mark against her family name because of Gail's impulsiveness.

Maybe she could at least explain the situation to someone before the news surfaced about Gail's lack of payment.

Scrolling back to the news piece, she found the name she was looking for. James Harris. The MC of the event must have been the one who'd tried contacting Gail. She'd missed seeing his photo in the margin of the story the first time, too dismayed by her sister's behavior to see beyond the text of the story. But now, Lydia's eyes lingered on the image of the man who was also the current president of the Texas Cattleman's Club.

Handsome didn't *begin* to describe him. The photo showed him in front of the organization's historic clubhouse building, a fawn-colored Stetson shielding his face from the Texas sun. Tall and well built, he wore a fitted gray jacket that skimmed impressive muscles. Broad where a man should be. Lean in the hips. An angular jaw with a great smile. She couldn't see his eyes clearly because they were shadowed by the brim of his hat, but his skin was a warm, inviting brown.

She blinked fast to banish the image from her brain since she could not afford to be sidelined by the man's potent sex appeal. Lydia was not in the market for romance. Her mother's active, dramatic love life had given Lydia a front-row seat for the way romance changed people. Fiona had metamorphosed into someone new for each guy she'd dated, heedless of how her whims affected the whole family. Lydia wasn't looking for even mild flirtation, *especially* not with someone her sister had bilked out of a small fortune.

She knew better than to try to fix things that were out of her control, but she could at least extend Mr. Harris the common courtesy of explaining Gail's situation. And, perhaps, learn possible options for compromise on the bill so she could speak sensibly to her sister upon her return. If she could still salvage some goodwill in the community in spite of Gail's fake bid, it would be a minor miracle.

Lydia had an appointment to meet with the contractor who was supposed to work on her kitchen at noon. But right after that, she'd stop by the Texas Cattleman's Club.

And hope with all her heart that James Harris was an understanding man.

"Lydia Walker is here to see you," the disembodied voice announced through James Harris's office intercom system.

He straightened from where he'd been practicing his golf swing in his office at the clubhouse. Although he'd never been much of a golfer, he had a golf tournament on his calendar and his competitive streak bristled at the idea of bringing down his foursome. Besides, focusing on a sport during his lunch break helped distract him from the knot of stress at the base of his spine. He'd never guessed the amount of work that came with his new position in the TCC, duties that ate into his time running his own ranch every day. But to complicate matters immeasurably, he now had a toddler nephew to raise.

When his brother, Parker, and Parker's wife had died in a car accident three months ago, James had been devastated. But in addition to his own grief at losing a loved one he'd deeply respected, he had been struggling with the fact that Parker's will entrusted James with the care of his son, Teddy. The weight of that responsibility threatened to take his knees out from under him if he allowed himself to dwell on it too long.

"Walker?" James repeated. The stress knot in

his back tightened more at the mention of his visitor's name. Setting aside the putter, he walked closer to the intercom. "As in the woman who ran off without paying her bachelor bid last week?"

How could someone publicly bid money they didn't have? Or maybe she did have the money, but she just didn't care to give the $100,000 she promised to the Pancreatic Cancer Research Foundation. Unwilling to risk the bad publicity, especially for an event he'd supervised, he'd ended up covering the debt himself. Better to keep the club out of the papers.

That didn't mean the matter was settled.

"That was *Gail* Walker." The woman at the desk out front lowered her voice. "Maybe Lydia is a relative."

"Send her in." He kicked two golf balls under the couch near the window. Lately, he didn't mind extending his hours on-site at the clubhouse since there was a child care facility in the building and it seemed the one place his nephew was content. At home, Teddy was a handful. And then some.

James strode toward his office door to greet his guest. He hoped she was carrying a big fat check. Because while James hadn't begrudged spending his personal funds on a worthy cause, he couldn't help but resent a woman who felt no obligation to uphold a social contract.

Pulling open the office door, he could see he'd startled the woman on the other side.

Tall and slim, she had light brown hair and honey-colored skin that set off wide hazel eyes. She was dressed in khakis and a neat white blouse with a long pink sweater belted at her waist. She had one hand raised as if to knock while she nibbled at her lush lower lip. Her gaze darted anxiously to his.

A wholly unexpected attraction blindsided him.

He stared at her a beat too long.

"Lydia Walker?" He offered his hand belatedly, irritated with himself for the wayward thoughts. "I'm James Harris."

"Nice to meet you." Her handshake was cool and firm. Businesslike. "Thank you for seeing me, Mr. Harris."

"Please, call me James." Standing back, he waved her into the office, leaving the door open to the club-house behind her. He glanced over toward the double doors leading into the child care facility, half expecting to see Teddy banging on the window. Or a child care worker running for the hills. But all was quiet. Thankfully. Returning his attention to his guest, he said, "Have a seat."

James gestured to one of the leather chairs near the windows overlooking the garden and swimming pool. The TCC president's office had been remodeled along with the rest of the historic building. Larger windows and higher ceilings now let in more light, and there were brighter colors in the decor. But the dark hardwood floors and oversize leather furnishings retained the feel of a men's club from a bygone era. Historic photographs and artifacts from the club's storied past filled the walls.

For a few hours here each week, he could pretend his life was normal again. That he wasn't a stand-in father struggling to provide a home for an eighteen-month-old boy who surely felt the absence of his parents, yet was far too young to express himself. Dragging his fractured thoughts back to the appealing woman in his office, James focused on the here and now.

"Can I get you something to drink, Ms. Walker? Coffee or tea? A water?"

"No, thank you. And please call me Lydia." She set her simple leather handbag on the floor by her feet while he lowered himself into the chair beside hers. "I won't take up much of your time. I just came to see what I could to do in regard to my sister's debt. I've been out of town, and I only just read the news this morning."

"Ah." He nodded, admiring her frank approach. "I appreciate that, Lydia, but I'm not sure how much I'm at liberty to divulge regarding your sister's... finances."

He was no expert in the law, but he felt sure that if Gail Walker hadn't specifically asked her sister to intervene on her behalf, he shouldn't discuss the woman's bad debt with her sibling.

"I'm not asking for any information." Lydia sat forward in her seat, her expression serious. "I already know that Gail couldn't possibly pay what she promised the charity on the night of the auction. I'm sure she will contact you when she returns from her trip. But until then, I wondered about a potential compromise."

So much for his hope that Lydia Walker came bearing a check.

"A compromise?" Impatience flared. He wasn't interested in a nominal payment toward the balance. "This isn't a credit card debt where you can take out a consolidation loan and suddenly pay less than you owe."

Lips compressed in a flat line, she straightened in her seat. "And I'm aware of that. But she can't produce funds she doesn't have. So I had hoped to give Gail some ideas for what she could do instead. Perhaps donate her time volunteering for the charity in some way?"

Her hazel eyes turned greener as she bristled. The color intrigued him, even as he knew he shouldn't take any pleasure from her frustration. She'd meant well.

"I see." He nodded, thinking over her offer. She didn't know that the charity had already been paid, but he wasn't sure he wanted to share his own contribution. Instead, he found himself asking, "May I ask your interest in the matter? Why not just let your sister contact us when she returns home?"

She arched an eyebrow. "Do you have any siblings, James?"

The question cut straight through him, his grief still fresh. "Not as of three months ago."

The terse sound of the words didn't begin to convey the ache behind them.

Lydia paled. "I'm so sorry. I had no idea—"

"You couldn't possibly know." Stuffing down the rawness of the loss, James stood suddenly, needing to move. He headed toward the minifridge and retrieved two small bottles of water, more for something to do than anything else. Still, he brought one back to Lydia and then cracked open his own. "My brother and his wife died in a car crash this fall. Parker lived on the other side of the state, but we were still close."

He had no living relatives now except for his nephew. His own mother had died of breast cancer when he was very young, and his father had passed after a heart attack two years ago. The Grim Reaper had been kicking him in the teeth lately, taking those he loved.

Except for Teddy. And James would move heaven and earth to keep that little hellion happy and safe. Even if it meant giving up the boy to his maternal grandparents—an option he was investigating since his schedule didn't allow the time the boy needed.

"I can't imagine how difficult that has been." The concern in her voice, the empathy, was unmistakable. "Most of my brothers and sisters are still back home in Arkansas, but I check in with them often. Gail moved here with me to—start over. I can't help but feel somewhat responsible for her."

He wondered why. Lured by curiosity about this beautiful woman, he almost sat back down beside her to continue their conversation. But a noise outside the office—the cadence of urgent voices speaking in low tones—distracted him from replying. He glanced toward the door that opened onto the clubhouse and saw the building's administrative assistant speaking with one of the women who worked in the child care facility.

A feeling of foreboding grew. He knew it couldn't be the boy's tree nut allergy acting up or they would have notified him. But what if Teddy had overstayed his welcome in the child care facility? James hadn't been able to keep a nanny for more than two weeks with his nephew's swings from shy and withdrawn to uncontrollable bouts of temper. James had no plan B if the TCC child care couldn't take the toddler for at least part of the time. The boy's only grandparents lived five hours away—too far for babysitting help.

"Lydia, you needn't worry about the donation,"

he told his guest, the stress at the base of his spine ratcheting higher up his back. As compelling as he found his unexpected guest, he needed to end this meeting so he could see what was going on with the boy. "I've already taken care of the matter with the charity, and I'll speak to your sister about it when she returns to Royal."

He remained standing, hoping his response would satisfy Lydia and send her on her way. Bad enough he'd felt an immediate attraction to the woman. But he was too strapped emotionally and mentally this week to figure out a creative solution to help her sister work off a debt that James had already paid.

"Taken care of?" Lydia sounded wary. "What does that mean?"

Tension throbbed in his temples. He would have never guessed that concerns about one tiny kid could consume a person day and night. But that's exactly where he found himself right now, worrying about the boy around the clock, certain that his lack of consistent care was going to screw up the child Parker had been so proud of.

"I paid off the bid myself," James clarified while he watched the child care worker edge around the administrative assistant and bustle toward his office door.

Damn it.

"You can't go in there," the front desk secretary called after her, while James waited, tension vibrating through him.

From behind him, Lydia Walker's gasp was followed by the whispered words, "One hundred thousand dollars?"

Damn it again.

Pivoting toward Lydia, he already regretted his haste. But he needed to concentrate on whatever new crisis was developing.

"That information is confidential, and stays between the two of us. I only shared it so you won't worry about the bid anymore."

Standing, Lydia gaped at him. She shook her head, the warm streaks in her brown hair glinting in the sunlight streaming through the windows behind her. "I'll worry twice as much now. How can we ever hope to repay you?"

He didn't have time to answer before a childish cry filled the room.

His nephew, little Teddy Harris, came barreling toward him with big crocodile tears running down both cheeks, his wispy baby curls bouncing with each jarring step. The two women stepped out of the boy's way as he ran straight into James's leg. Crushing the wool gabardine in damp baby hands, the boy let out a wail that all of Royal must have heard.

With proof of his inadequacy as a stand-in parent clinging to his calf, James had never felt so powerless. Reaching down, he lifted his nephew in his arms to offer whatever comfort he could, knowing it wasn't going to be enough. The toddler thrashed in his arms, his back arching, kicking with sock-clad feet.

James had all he could do to hang on to the squirming kid let alone soothe him.

Until, miraculously, the child stilled. The two women lingering at the threshold of his office door were both smiling as they watched. James had to crane his neck to see the boy's expression since Teddy peered at something over his shoulder, tantrum forgotten.

For a split second, he wondered what on earth that could be. Until he remembered the enticing woman in the room with them.

He sensed her presence behind him in a hint of feminine fragrance and a soft footfall on the hardwood floor. It was James's only warning, before her voice whispered, "peekaboo!" in a way that tickled against his left ear.

Teddy erupted in giggles.

It was, without question, the best magic trick James had ever witnessed. And he knew immediately that there was a way Ms. Lydia Walker could repay him.

Two

Once the child in James's arms had settled down, the Texas Cattleman's Club's handsome president set the boy on his feet while he went to speak in low tones to the two women who hovered near the entrance of his office.

Lydia did her best not to eavesdrop even though she was wildly curious about the identity of the toddler. The brief bio she'd read of James online hadn't mentioned a wife or family, and he didn't wear a wedding ring. Not that it was any of her business. But clearly, the child was his based on the way the toddler had flung chubby arms around James's leg like he was home base in a game of tag.

For that matter, they shared the same brown eyes flecked with gold, as well.

A gentle tug on the sleeve of her sweater made Lydia realize she'd gotten sidetracked during this round of "peekaboo." She glanced back to the sober little boy in front of her, his damp hand clutching the ribbed cuff of her sweater to help him keep balance. He looked sleepy and out of sorts as he wobbled on unsteady legs, but the game was still entertaining him. Obediently, she covered her face to hide again, remembering how much her youngest brother had loved playing.

"Thank you," James said to the woman from the front desk. "I'll take care of it."

Then he turned and walked back toward Lydia.

She watched him through her fingers as she hid her face from Teddy. Tall and lean, James Harris moved with the grace of an athlete even in jeans and boots. His button-down shirt looked custom fitted, the only giveaway to his position at the club. Without the Stetson he'd been wearing in the photo she'd seen of him online, she could now appreciate the golden color of his eyes. His dark hair was close cropped, the kind of cut that meant regular trips to the barber. Everything about him was neat. Well-groomed. Incredibly good-looking.

The sight of him was enough to make her throat dry right up in feminine appreciation. She might have forgotten all about the peekaboo game if

Teddy hadn't patted her knee. Belatedly, she slid her hands from her face and surprised the toddler again.

The boy giggled softly before resting his head on her knee, as though he was too tired to hold himself upright any longer. Poor little guy. She rubbed his back absently while the baby fidgeted with his feet.

"I think he'll be down for the count in another minute," she told James quietly. "He's an adorable child."

"He's normally a handful," James admitted, taking the seat across from her. "You're very good with him."

His charming smile made her breath hitch in her chest. James Harris's photo online hadn't fully prepared her for how devastatingly sexy he'd be in person, an attraction she had no business feeling for a man who had a family of his own. A man who'd bailed her sister out of a thorny financial mess that could have very well derailed both their careers. How could Lydia ever thank him?

"As the oldest of eight kids, I had a lot of first-hand experience," she admitted, accustomed to glossing over the hurtful aspects of feeling more like hired help than her mother's daughter. "I've worked as a nanny ever since and I hope to open my own child care business out of my home this year." It couldn't hurt to start spreading the word to people in the community with young families. "Do you have any other children?"

The question sounded benign enough, right? Not like she was fishing to find out more about whether or not this handsome man was married with a house full of adorable offspring waiting to greet him at the end of the day.

"No." A shadowed expression crossed his face. "Teddy is my brother's son. And up until Teddy's parents died three months ago, I was a bachelor spending every waking hour running a ranch or performing my duties here. My life has been turned upside down."

She couldn't deny the momentary relief that James was single. But just as quickly, she thought of the sadness and weariness in his voice and what that meant for Teddy. Her heart ached for all the little boy had lost. She stared down at him, his soft cheek still resting on her knee while he shifted his weight from one foot to the other, his light-up sneakers flashing back and forth at odd intervals while he rocked.

"I'm so sorry." She smoothed a palm across the back of the boy's gray dinosaur T-shirt. "For you both. I can't imagine how difficult that transition has been to deal with, especially when you're grieving such a tragic loss."

She glanced back at James to find him studying her.

His fixed attention rattled her, reminding her that he'd just admitted to being a single man. Warmth rose to her cheeks and she looked away, trying to remember the thread of the conversation.

"You could help us immeasurably." James's voice was pitched low in deference to the weary baby between them, but the tone made her think of pillow talk. Intimate conversations between two lovers who knew one another incredibly well.

Who would have guessed a whisper could be so seductive?

"I'm—um." She tried to think beyond murmured confidences and came up blank, her brain already supplying images of tangled sheets and limbs. "And how would that be?"

"You arrived at my door looking for a compromise on your sister's bid, and we've just found the perfect one." He pointed to Teddy, who had stopped moving, his eyes closed. Breathing even. "If you'll take the job of Teddy's nanny, you can consider Gail's debt paid in full."

His suggestion staggered her. Called her from her sensual daydreams.

"She bid *one hundred thousand dollars*," Lydia reminded him, wondering where she should lay Teddy down for a nap. "You'd be forgiving the cost of a home for the sake of child care. That's far too generous of you."

He shook his head, his jaw flexing. "I haven't

kept a nanny for more than two weeks because he's
such a handful, between the tantrums and days of
being withdrawn. We could have a trial period to
see how it worked out." He seemed to warm to the
idea quickly, laying out terms. "If you stayed for a
trial period of two months, then I'd forgive half the
debt. Stick around for a year, and we'll call it even."

"You can't be serious." She got distracted around
him after a few minutes. How could she ever work
in his home for a year?

"I'm running out of options and I can't afford
this much time away from my ranching business.
You have no idea what it would be worth to me to
know my brother's boy is in good hands."

She couldn't miss the desperation in his eyes.
In his voice. But as much as she felt called to help
him, it wasn't her debt to pay. Gail was the one
who should be providing free nanny services, not
her. Still, another thought trickled through, making her realize things weren't quite so simple. No
matter how strongly she felt that Gail needed to
clean up her own messes, Lydia recognized that
without James's clearing the debt with the charity,
the Walker name might have become the kiss of
death for a new business in a close-knit community like Royal. While she wrestled with what to
do, she turned her attention to the sleeping baby
between them.

"First things first, we should find a comfortable place for Teddy." She reached to lift him, but James moved closer.

"I can get him." He slipped his hands around the boy's waist to pick him up, his hand briefly brushing against her calf and causing a whole riot of sensations in her before he shifted the child to rest on his shoulder. "And you don't need to make a decision about my offer right now. If you're okay with continuing our meeting another time, I should be leaving for the day anyhow. I think he'll stay asleep if I put him in his car seat."

Lydia tried to ignore the residual tingling in her skin. She appreciated the opportunity he was giving her to think about his proposal. And distance from his striking good looks would give her the chance to think with a clearer head.

"You have someone to watch him today?" Lydia didn't mean to sound like she was questioning his arrangements for the child. She was just trying to keep the focus on Teddy and not the heady jolt of attraction she was feeling.

She stood to follow James toward the door.

"My foreman's daughter is home from college for the holidays, and she agreed to give me afternoon help two days a week for the next month. That's as much child care as I've got covered when I'm not here. Provided she doesn't give up on Teddy, too, when he has his next atomic meltdown." He sounded frustrated and she understood why.

James shouldered the leather diaper bag that the child care worker had set near the door to his office, then lifted his Stetson from the coat rack and dropped it into place. When she stepped out of the room, he locked the door behind them. She couldn't miss the way his large hands cradled the child so gently against his broad chest. The gesture called to her, reminding her of dreams she had for her own children one day.

Not that she was thinking of James in that way. She must be overtired and stressed to let her imagination wander like that. The sooner she made tracks out of here and away from James's tempting presence, the better.

As they left the clubhouse and strode out into the December sunlight, James tugged a blanket from an exterior pocket of the diaper bag and laid it over the sleeping boy. The day was mild, but with the holidays approaching, the temperatures had been dropping. Lydia tipped her face into the breeze, grateful for the cooler air on her too-warm skin.

"I researched the child care facilities in town when I got the idea to open a full-service business here, and I know there's a definite need." Royal was thriving, and the demographics for young families were a particular area of growth. "I've heard there are waiting lists at the most coveted places."

James nodded in response. "You've got that right. When I called one day care they said families reserve space when they're pregnant, even knowing they might not put a child into the system for a full year." He sighed wearily. "The last few months have been an education—from learning how to change a diaper to educating myself on how to avoid tree nuts for his allergy."

"He has allergies?" Lydia was accustomed to the dietary needs for children with the most common allergies. Her brother broke out in hives if he even got in the same room as a peanut.

"Just tree nuts. But I live in fear I'll leave the house without the EpiPen." He huffed out a long breath, clearly feeling the same stress that many new parents went through. "I hope you'll consider my offer, Lydia. Maybe you can work for me, and your sister can do something to repay you."

"I'd need to figure out a way to pay my bills in the meantime." It was true she was between nanny jobs right now, but she had hoped to devote the extra time toward working on her house, doing some of the simpler labor she didn't want to pay a contractor for.

James tucked the blanket more securely around the baby's feet, a gesture that touched her all the more now that she knew he wasn't the baby's father. He was simply a man trying to do his best taking care of a child he hadn't been ready for.

"And I can't put a price on what it would mean to me to have qualified help with Teddy." He nodded at a gray-haired cowboy walking into the club. Then, once the man had passed, James turned to Lydia again. "Forget about Gail and the charity money. The universe is smiling on me by having a nanny walk into my office at a time in my life when I'm hanging on by my fingernails. Consider this a job offer for whatever you usually charge. I would have sought you out before this if I'd known about you."

"I couldn't possibly—"

"Please." He cut her off, his tone laced with an urgency—a need—she hadn't anticipated. "Just think about it. Start with the trial period and sign on for two months. See how it goes. If things don't work out, I'll understand."

Swallowing her protests, she nodded. "It's a very generous offer and I will consider it."

He seemed to relax then, a tension sliding away from him as he exhaled. "Thank you. I'll be working from the main house at the Double H tomorrow. If you'd like to stop by, I can show you around. You could see what the job would entail and take a look at the nanny's quarters before you decide."

"The Double H is your ranch?" She knew the property. It was close to the Clayton family ranch, the Silver C. The portions of the Double H she could see from the main road were all beautifully manicured. The stables and ranch house were both painted crisp white with dark gray trim, and the window boxes were refreshed year-round with red flowers.

"It is." His smile was warm. "I never knew how easy ranch work was until I tried my hand at child care. I'm very ready to return to my cattle full-time."

The idea troubled her, given that his responsibility to his nephew wasn't going to end when he filled the nanny position. But she couldn't afford to feel any more empathy for this man than she already did. She had some tough decisions ahead of her where he was concerned.

"I'll stop by tomorrow. Does after lunch work for you?"

"That's perfect." He laid a protective hand on Teddy's back. "You can repeat the trick you did today of getting him to fall asleep for his nap."

She'd been given similar compliments many times from happy clients. She was good with children. Period. And yet, somehow the thought of putting the child to sleep with James Harris looking on filled her with a whole host of fluttery sensations.

"I'll see you then." Nodding, she backed away fast, needing refuge from the strong pull of desire. Retreating to her car, she forced her gaze away from James and shut the door behind her.

She locked the door for good measure. And then felt like an idiot if he'd heard her flick the locks. She wasn't trying to keep anyone out as much as she was trying to keep herself in check around the too-handsome rancher with golden-brown eyes.

Switching on the ignition, she pulled out of the parking lot fast, hating herself for thinking that if it wasn't for James's blatant sex appeal, she probably already would have accepted the job he'd offered.

That wasn't fair to him. And it definitely wasn't fair to the innocent boy who'd just lost both his parents.

She could help Teddy and James. And no matter what she told herself about not getting involved in her sister's mayhem, Lydia felt a responsibility to repay James in whatever way she could. By covering Gail's debt, he'd ensured both Walker women would be able to run their small businesses in Royal without censure from locals knowing that Gail had cheated the Pancreatic Cancer Research Foundation.

Lydia would just have to find a way to do the job while avoiding the hot rancher as much as possible.

Shouldering the pole pruner he'd been using to trim an apple tree, James squinted in the afternoon sunlight to check his watch at half-past noon.

Based on the number of times he'd glanced at the vintage Omega Seamaster timepiece that had belonged to his grandfather, James couldn't deny that he looked forward to a visit from Lydia Walker today. And as much as he wanted to credit his anticipation to the possibility he'd found a solution to his nanny problem, he knew that accounted for only part of it.

He wanted to see her again.

Taking his time to wipe down the blade on the pruner—an important step to prevent spreading disease—James needed to be sure Lydia agreed to his bargain. And frankly, that need was at odds with how fiercely he was attracted to her. She'd invaded his thoughts constantly since their last meeting. During the daytime, he shut down the visions as fast as possible. But during the night? His dreams about her had been wildly inappropriate and hot as hell.

Securing a nanny was his number one goal right now, and had been for the past three months. He couldn't afford to let an undeniable hunger for her confuse the issue that should be a simple business arrangement. Her sister's overbid aside, James needed Lydia. He'd spent time the night before researching her credentials and had been thoroughly impressed. Not only had she served as a nanny for two TCC members who spoke highly of her—he'd messaged them both to check—but Lydia also had an intriguing connection to the popular childrearing blog *House Rules*.

The blog was written by her mother, Fiona, but had often featured Lydia even as a teenager. There was a whole video library of Lydia, showing her mother's followers how to do everything from making organic baby food to refreshing vintage nursery furniture to meeting modern health codes. Simply put, she was incredibly qualified. But the most convincing fact for him was that he'd seen how quickly she could turn Teddy's stormy tantrums into full-fledged smiles.

That alone made her services necessary. And he'd be damned if he allowed his unbidden desire for the woman to get in the way. Besides, if his divorce had taught him anything, it was that chemistry between people could fade fast, and made shaky ground for any relationship.

Heading toward the potting shed to stow the garden tools, James heard the crunch of car tires on gravel. Turning, he recognized Lydia's vehicle from the day before. He made quick work of putting away the tools and washed his hands at the shed's utility sink before stepping outside again.

He had almost reached her car when she stepped from it. Her long legs were clad in tall boots and dark leggings. A gray sweater dress and long herringbone-patterned coat were simple, efficient pieces. Definitely nothing overtly sexy. And yet, he found his gaze wandering over the way the sweater dress hugged her curves. But it was her smile that drew him more than anything. From her light brown hair streaked with honey to the sun-warmed shade of her skin, she seemed to glow from within. Today, like yesterday, she wore little makeup that he could see. A long golden necklace glinted as she straightened, the charms jingling gently as they settled.

"Welcome to the Double H," he greeted her, arms spread wide. "Home of the Harris family since nine-teen fifty-three."

He and his brother had been born here and he took immense pride in the place, the same as his father had before his death. His brother had planned to move back to Royal one day and help expand the ranching operation. A plan that would never hap-pen now. Strange how many ways grief could find to stab him when he least expected it.

Still, James continued to think about expanding on his own, to give Teddy the future that his father had dreamed for him.

"Thank you." She let him close the car door be-hind her while she spun in a slow circle to view the closest buildings. "I've always thought this was a pretty property when I've driven past here."

He couldn't help the rueful grin. "I don't know how thrilled my grandfather would be to hear that I've turned the place 'pretty.' But I've toyed with the idea of expanding the horse sales side of the business after we've had some success with re-cent yearlings. And traditionally, horse farms have more curb appeal since potential clients often come through the barns."

"You've done a great job." Lydia walked toward the small grove where he'd been working. "Are these fruit trees?"

He nodded, pleased she'd noticed. "I've got a dozen apple trees, a few peaches and pears. Just enough to make the ranch hands grumble about the extra work at harvest time." Although no one complained about taking fresh fruit home at the end of the day. "I was pruning these before you arrived."

"I hope I didn't catch you at a bad time." She stopped her trek through the grove and peered back at him. "I know I'm a little early, but I wasn't sure how long the drive would take."

"I had just quit when you pulled in. Your timing is perfect." He waved her toward a side entrance to the main house. "Come on in. Can I get you something to drink?"

"No. Thank you." She waited while he opened the door, then stepped inside the mudroom. "Where's Teddy? I brought him a gift." She tugged at the sleeve of her coat and he moved behind her to help.

Her hair brushed the backs of his knuckles, the silk lining of her coat warm from her body. He tried to move quickly—to keep himself from lingering too long—but he wasn't fast enough to avoid a hint of her fragrance. Something vanilla with a trace of floral.

With effort, he turned away from her to hang the coat on one of the metal hooks from the rack.

"That's very kind of you. My housekeeper took Teddy for a couple of hours while he naps so I could get the trees sprayed and pruned. I've been falling behind on every conceivable chore." He led her deeper into the house, pausing outside the kitchen. "Besides, I wanted to give my sales pitch for the nanny gig without any distraction."

Shaking her head, she gave him a half smile. "But *he* is the job, James. Your best selling point."

Skeptical, he figured he'd hedge his bets on showing off the house first. "Your three predecessors didn't seem quite as charmed by their charge."

Lydia crossed her arms as she studied him. "They don't sound worthy of the task, then."

Her defensiveness on Teddy's behalf was a credit to her character, yes. But she'd been with the boy for only a few minutes. She hadn't seen the long crying jags or the stormy rages that had caught the other nannies off guard.

"That makes me all the more eager to sign you on," he told her honestly.

After taking her on a tour of the kitchen and great room, he took the main staircase up to the nursery where his housekeeper, Mrs. Davis, all but bolted from the room when she spotted them. Her greeting was brusque at best.

"Thank you, Mrs. Davis." James knew the housekeeper wasn't happy with the added babysitting responsibilities, but he'd shown his gratitude in her paycheck over the last two weeks. "This is Lydia Walker. She's here to discuss the possibility of taking over child care duties full-time."

"In that case, I won't keep you." She gave an abrupt nod and hurried on her way, her white tennis shoes squeaking on the hardwood in the hall as she stalked off.

"The household staff is overburdened," he explained, hoping Lydia wouldn't be put off by the woman's cool reception. "Mrs. Davis has helped me out more than once, and I've also got temporary help from my foreman's daughter. But the extra work is taking a toll."

"Understandable," Lydia murmured softly while she peered down into the crib at the sleeping baby. "Caring for a child is a huge life adjustment. Expectant parents have nine months to prepare themselves, and most of them are still overwhelmed by the transition." She smiled up at him. "You're doing well."

No doubt she intended the words to be reassuring, but the effect on him was anything but.

"You can't possibly know that," he told her flatly, refusing to accept a comfort he didn't deserve. "I can't help but think that my brother would have been far more involved with his son's upbringing than I can afford to be right now. I've reached out to Teddy's maternal grandparents to try to involve them more." He'd written to them twice, in fact, and hadn't heard back. "Maybe their home will be a better place for my nephew."

Lydia chewed her lush lower lip, looking thoughtful. The gesture distracted him from the dark cloud of his own failed responsibilities, making him wish his relationship with this woman could be a whole lot less complicated.

"You're thinking about asking his grandparents to raise him?" She stepped away from the crib, her boots soundless on the thick carpeting as she moved.

His gaze tracked her movements, lingering on the way her sweater dress hugged her curves. But then, thinking about Lydia was a whole lot more enticing than remembering all the ways he'd fallen short in his sudden parental role.

He'd had the nursery assembled in a hurry. The room contained all the necessary furniture but hadn't been decorated with much that would appeal to a child.

"Definitely. I can't even keep a nanny for him, let alone be a meaningful part of his life right now." He wasn't sure any of this was helping his cause to convince her to take the job. But something about Lydia made it easy for him to talk to her.

A sensation he rarely experienced with anyone.

"But that doesn't mean you'll always be too

busy for him." Her hazel eyes took on a bluish cast in the baby's room with azure-colored walls. "And your brother and his wife must have trusted you a great deal if they named you as his guardian."

Frustration and guilt fired through him.

"I'm sure they never believed it would come to that." He couldn't bear the weight of failing Teddy. Failing his brother. Unwilling to argue the point, James gestured toward the door. "Come this way and I'll show you the nanny's quarters. Because no matter what happens with Teddy's future, I can't escape the fact that I need a solution for his care right now."

And that meant not letting his guard down around this beautiful, desirable woman.

Three

"I can't accept these terms." Back in the ranch's great room, Lydia stared down at the neatly typed offer James had passed her inside a crisp manila folder.

After a tour of the Double H Ranch main house, with special attention to the nursery, nanny's quarters and a potential playroom she could equip as she saw fit, James had briefly outlined very generous compensation for retaining her services. Not only was room and board included—useful for her while her contractor outfitted her home for a child care facility—but James also offered a salary, health care benefits and a recommendation if she stayed in his employ for six months. Gail's debt would be partially forgiven after the two-month trial period, and fully after one whole year.

Furthermore, there were additional pages that spelled out potential budgets for renovating the playroom and nursery, as well as a spending allowance for toys, books, equipment, outings and anything else that she thought Teddy required.

"What do you mean?" James frowned, stepping closer to glance over her shoulder at the formalized offer he'd given her. "Are there things I'm overlooking? It's all up for negotiation."

Closing the folder, she passed it back to him as they stood in front of the huge stone hearth where a fire crackled. "You haven't overlooked a thing. This is far too generous."

She'd never heard of such a well-paid nanny. And it made her heart hurt to think he was so eager to give over the boy's care that he would pay someone such an inflated fee. Especially when he was debating relinquishing the child to Teddy's maternal grandparents.

"Honoring my brother's wishes means everything to me." His jaw flexed as raw emotion flashed in his eyes, but he folded his arms, as if defying her to argue that statement.

"I understand that." Truly, she did. "But the whole reason I came to see you yesterday was to discuss options for repaying your generosity toward my sister. I can't let you give us anything else."

He was shaking his head before she even finished speaking. "You can't sacrifice your own income for the sake of your sibling. I won't hear of it." Before she could argue, he continued, "I read about you online, Lydia. You're extremely qualified."

His words pleased her. Or maybe it was the knowledge that he'd spent time thinking of her, if only in a professional capacity. Warmth crawled over her that didn't have a thing to do with the fire.

"Thank you. I already have a health care plan, so I don't need that. But if you cut the salary in half, I would be amenable."

"Half?" He shook his head. "I couldn't look myself in the mirror if you took a nickel under three-quarters of that."

"Half," she insisted. "And I'll find a way to put my sister to work for me so she's making up the difference."

Gail needed to learn that there were consequences to her impulsive actions.

He scrubbed a hand through his close-cropped dark hair. "I don't know."

She suspected he would have continued to argue the figure if a wail from the nursery hadn't sounded at that precise moment. James's gaze went to the staircase.

"I could start immediately," she offered, sensing his weakening on the salary issue.

He extended his hand. "You've got yourself a deal."

Lydia slipped her small palm into his much larger one, seized with the memory of their brief contact the day before when he'd taken Teddy from her arms. Just like then, an electric current seemed to jump between them, hot to the point of melting. Her gaze met his, and she would swear he was aware of it, too.

She was grateful for the baby's next cry, since it gave her the perfect excuse to retract her fingers. She darted from the room to escape the temptation of her new boss—and the fear that she'd just made a huge mistake.

After a brief supper shared with her new charge in the nursery, Lydia debated the wisdom of starting her new job so quickly.

She'd jumped into the baby's routine with both feet, comfortable with knowing where most things were located since her new employer had given her a quick tour. She knew the protocol for Teddy's food allergies and where the EpiPens were kept. But she hadn't clarified how or when she would go about moving her things into her suite at the Double H, thinking she'd see her new boss at dinnertime.

But James still hadn't come in from his chores at eight o'clock after she put Teddy into his crib for the night. Lydia knew because she'd peered down the stairs a few times, and twice had checked in with the housekeeper.

On both occasions, Mrs. Davis had looked at her as though she might steal the house silver at any moment. And between the woman's terse answers and general lack of hospitality, Lydia had the distinct impression that her presence was not welcomed by the older housekeeper.

Not that she was too worried. Usually, her work spoke for itself. Maybe Mrs. Davis was simply tired from the strain of caring for a little one. Lydia was more concerned to think that James might not be accessible in the coming weeks. As Teddy's parental figure, James had an important role in the boy's life even if he hadn't fully committed himself to it yet.

Then again, maybe James's disappearing act had nothing to do with his nephew and everything to do with the blossoming attraction between them.

Figuring she'd never improve things around here if she stayed hidden in her room, Lydia stepped out of the sprawling nanny suite and hurried down the hall to the staircase. The natural wood banister was polished to a high sheen, and the house's log cabin elements mingled seamlessly with more contemporary touches, like the walls painted in shades of taupe and tan. Downstairs, the stone hearth rose to a high ceiling right through the upstairs gallery walkway. A rough wood mantel and steer horns decorated the fireplace, but the leather couches and cream-colored slipper chairs were sleekly styled and inviting. Agriculture books filled the shelves in the far corner of the room, the leather spines freshly dusted.

She peered around for any signs of Mrs. Davis but didn't see the housekeeper. Before Lydia could debate her next move, the side door opened and James stepped inside.

She stood far enough away that he didn't notice her at first. He took his time hanging his Stetson and shrugging out of a weatherproof duster. Belatedly, she felt a hint of cool air that must have entered the house with him. The temperature had dropped, and she knew a storm was predicted tonight. In the shadows of the mudroom, his features looked all the more sculpted. He had high cheekbones. A strong jaw. Well-muscled shoulders that would turn any woman's head.

And yes, she acknowledged, she liked looking at him.

"Do you always work so late?" she asked as a way to reveal her presence, feeling suddenly self-conscious.

He glanced up quickly, his expression more pleased than surprised.

"Hello, Lydia. I didn't expect to see you so late."

She glanced at the antique clock on the opposite wall. "It's not even nine."

"Right. And when I've been on duty with my nephew, I'm ready for bed before he is." He toed off his boots and lined them up on the far side of the welcome mat.

There was something oddly intimate about seeing him take off his shoes. Being in his home at this hour.

Which was a silly thing to think given that she'd been a nanny before. She'd seen parents moving around their living space while she helped out with children. Maybe it felt different with James because he was single.

And…smoking hot. Her gaze tracked him as he strode into the kitchen in sock feet. In a long-sleeved gray tee and dark jeans, he looked less like the polished Texas Cattleman's Club president and more like a ruggedly handsome rancher. He scrubbed his hands at the kitchen sink.

"Teddy went to bed fairly well for me." So far, she couldn't see any evidence of the toddler being more difficult than most children his age. "Beginner's luck, maybe."

"Or maybe you're just that good." He grinned at her while he dried off, her thoughts scrambling at the mild flirtation in the words. "Would you like to join me for dinner? I'm starving, but I'd appreciate hearing more about your day."

He moved toward the stainless steel refrigerator and tugged it open.

"No, thank you. Teddy and I ate dinner earlier." She couldn't risk spending too much time in her employer's presence based on her over-the-top physical reaction to just a handshake, for crying out loud. If she was going to reach at least the two-month mark on this trial period, she really shouldn't have late meals alone with him. "I just thought maybe now would be a good time for me to return to my house and pick up a few items to get me through the next week."

"I forgot you didn't move your things in today." He backed out of the refrigerator with a sandwich on a crusty French roll and proceeded to remove the clear plastic wrap. "There's a storm brewing that could turn nasty if the temperature drops any more."

"I'll be careful." She stepped closer to the kitchen but didn't enter it, remaining outside the granite-topped breakfast bar as she watched him retrieve a plate and glass. "I can be back in two hours."

He parted the curtain on the window over the kitchen sink, peering out into the night. "The roads are going to be dangerous if we get ice."

"As the oldest of eight in my family, I have to say it's a unique experience to have someone worry about my safety for a change." She couldn't help a rueful smile, since she was usually the one doing the worrying.

"What about your mom?" he asked, letting go of the sheer curtain to fill a water glass. "She didn't ever tell you not to go out into an ice storm?"

Even with the barrier of the counter between them, she felt the draw of his curiosity about her. She'd never experienced the pinprick of awareness all over her skin with anyone else and wondered why, of all the people Gail could have indebted herself to, it had to be a man whom Lydia found so potently sexy.

"My mother doesn't take much notice of potential dangers in the environment." To put it mildly. Lydia had saved her youngest sister from drowning in a neighbor's backyard pool while her mom led a workshop on fostering a love of Mother Earth in children. She'd been totally oblivious. "Fiona Walker truly believes that if you see hearts and flowers wherever you go, then the world must be a happy, safe place."

James's eyebrows lifted as he slid his sandwich into the microwave. "Sounds like you got to see a different side of the *House Rules* parenting approach."

She wasn't surprised he knew about the blog. Her mother's PR machine regularly spit out stats about how many lives the parenting website actively changed for the better—which was their highly embroidered way of reporting social media reach.

Choosing her words carefully, she replied, "Let's

just say that I hope you didn't hire me because you thought I'd be giving Teddy lessons in the power of positive thinking."

"Honestly, I was just happy to read that you have CPR certification along with good references and a clean driving record." He withdrew his meal from the microwave. "But how about you let me drive you to pick up your things and we'll talk about your first day on the way?"

"What about Teddy?"

"Mrs. Davis will hear him if he cries." He picked up a key ring from a dish on the granite countertop. "Besides, we'll be back before he wakes."

She needed to speak to him about that. It didn't make her comfortable to leave her young charge in the care of a woman who seemed to resent having to watch over him. But chances were good— even if she insisted on driving herself—that James would let his housekeeper tend the child if Teddy woke anyhow.

Somehow, she had to help James feel more comfortable in a father role. And no matter that the close proximity of a car ride with her strikingly handsome boss might prove tempting, Lydia knew the sooner she discussed those issues with him, the better.

"Okay. Let me just get the nursery monitor set up for her." She had the baby monitor feed on her phone, but she knew the model in the nursery came with a physical receiver.

James nodded as he pulled out his phone. "Take your time. I'll finish up my meal while you do that." He scrolled through his screens. "Mrs. Davis's room is the first one on the left just downstairs. You can leave the monitor outside her door and I'll text her the plan. She doesn't go to sleep until after the late news anyhow."

Lydia walked upstairs to the nursery, hurrying in spite of James's assurance they could take their time. Teddy Harris had been through enough these last few months. The quicker they went, the sooner Lydia would be back here, minimizing the chance that the child would wake up to Mrs. Davis.

After retrieving the receiver, she paused near the baby's crib, gazing at his little face in the glow of a night-light. So angelic. His rosebud mouth slightly open, his fingers clutching a soft rattle in the shape of a blue puppy dog.

Tenderness filled her as she closed the door quietly behind her. Somehow, some way, she would get through at least the next two months. Not just for the way it would help Gail.

She knew she could make a difference in the baby's life. And, she hoped, in his uncle's, too.

Windshield wipers working double time, James focused on the road ahead as he navigated his pickup truck down the quiet county road that led to Lydia's place. He'd eaten enough dinner to take the edge off one hunger, but having his nephew's new nanny beside him stirred another.

He tried his damnedest not to think about that. But with her light vanilla fragrance teasing his nose when she leaned closer to switch the radio station away from some political news, he couldn't resist the urge to drag in a deep breath.

"There." She leaned back in the passenger seat once a steel guitar sounded through the surround-sound speakers. "I hope that's okay. I hate to shirk my civic duty, but some days I can't cope with even one more story about politics."

"Rainy nights and steel guitars go hand in hand." He glanced over at her profile in the reflected light of the dashboard. "But then, you're talking to a man with a lot of Texas in his blood."

"Is that right?"

He heard the smile in her voice, even with his eyes back on the road and the glare of another vehicle's bright lights.

"Yes, ma'am. My granddaddy was born on Galveston Island, but he moved here after the Korean War when an army buddy of his died and left him the care of his family farm."

"Your grandfather inherited the Double H?" She shifted her legs toward him, her knees not all that far from his.

For a moment, he cursed the size of his truck. If they'd taken her car, her leg would be brushing up against him right now. But then, he recalled that he was not supposed to be imagining his legs entwined with hers. He had no business thinking about an employee that way.

"The land wasn't really a ranch at that time. Just some farm acreage. His friend's widow was struggling to raise three kids and get the crops in, so Henry Harris Sr. moved into a trailer on the land and got to work." He'd heard the story from his father often enough, since his granddad had passed away when James was still a child.

"My house is up here on the left." She pointed to a turn ahead. "I'm sure your grandfather would be proud of how you're maintaining the property. It's a showplace."

Her words pleased him. He'd worked tirelessly for the last ten years to modernize.

"Thank you." He slowed the vehicle as he guided it into the horseshoe driveway in front of a single-story residence. Concrete-block built, the white house had what appeared to be building materials neatly stacked under tarps in the front yard. "Looks like you've got some improvements planned yourself."

"Not as quickly as I would like, but yes." She pointed toward a portico structure on the far side of the building. "If you want to park under there, we can get inside without getting too drenched."

Moments later, he followed her inside, the rain

battering hard on the portico roof as she jiggled her key in a stubborn lock. He noticed the overhang leaked in a few places, with rivulets of water streaming through the gaps.

Inside, she flipped on a light to reveal a home in transit. Plastic sheeting hung on one end of a functional kitchen, an attempt to keep dust at a minimum, he guessed. But the workable section of living space that he could see showed tidy counters and cabinets, a big worktable covered with flooring samples and countertop tiles.

Beyond that, there were small touches of the woman who lived here. A bright braided rug. Heart-shaped magnets on the refrigerator that pinned a child's crayon art in places of honor. A small wall shelf contained a collection of glass and ceramic birds.

"I'll just be a minute." She headed toward an overlapping section of the plastic sheeting that divided the living space. "I need to grab some clothes."

"Can I carry anything for you?" He studied her in the light of a wrought iron chandelier over the kitchen table. "There's plenty of room in the extended cab if you want to bring any furniture or personal items to make you feel more at home."

"I don't need much—" She hesitated. "Actually, I have a few toys that Teddy might like if you want to come with me."

She held the plastic sheeting open for him and he ducked through, passing close to her. Brushing her shoulder with his accidentally. Was it his imagination, or did she suck in a breath at the contact?

He stopped too close to her in the small space, but a temporary wall had been constructed of plywood, making the hallway narrow here.

"Sorry about the mess," she said, quickly stepping ahead of him. "I've been living in a construction zone. I hardly notice it anymore when it's just me here."

His gaze roved—without his permission—to the sultry curve of her hips in her khaki slacks as she strode ahead of him. She paused to flip a light switch on one wall, and then she turned into what looked like a storage area.

"I'm glad to help," he told her honestly, not wanting to admit how much he liked spending time with her. How content he would be to linger with her here.

"Do you want to pull down those two suitcases?" she asked, pivoting in her tennis shoes to face him.

He hoped he'd lifted his gaze to eye level fast enough.

Damn. What the hell was he thinking to ogle her?

"Sure thing." He skirted around a couple of box fans to the shelves that held the luggage, and pulled down the items she'd indicated.

While he did that, she dug in a big box filled

with plastic scooters, ride-on toys and trucks. He resisted the view of her tempting feminine form, concentrating on opening the first suitcase like his life depended on it.

He steeled himself for the inevitable draw of her proximity when he brought the bag over to her. In short order, she tossed in a farm set with clear plastic bags full of toy animals, fencing and tractors. She added a few other items he didn't recognize—baby gear of some sort.

"You know you can buy whatever you think he needs—"

"Babies outgrow things so quickly. It makes more sense to share." Their eyes met over the suitcase he held.

He studied her, forgetting what they'd been talking about as sparks singed between them. For a moment, they breathed in one another's air. And from the protracted pause, he knew she was as distracted by the sizzling connection as he was.

If she was any other woman, he would have set aside the suitcase and pulled her into his arms. Tested her lips to see if they were as petal soft as they looked. Wrapped his arms around her curves to see if she fit against him as perfectly as he imagined she would.

He could practically hear his own heartbeat. It rushed in time with her fast breathing in the otherwise silent room.

What he wouldn't give for just one taste…

"I'd better get my clothes," she said suddenly, pulling him out of his thoughts just in time for him to see her rush out the door and disappear down the hall.

Cursing himself up one side and down the other, James zipped the suitcase and carried it back out to the safety of the empty kitchen.

As he waited for Lydia to finish, he ground his teeth together and reminded himself that the luggage wasn't the only thing that needed to stay zipped.

Four

As the holidays neared, Lydia put all her focus on
setting up happy daily routines for Teddy Harris.

She was good at her job, after all, and she needed
to have something in her life that was working in
her favor when she felt like she was tempted by
her boss every time she turned around. Not that
either of them had acknowledged the almost-kiss
that happened nearly two weeks ago on the night
he'd driven her to her home.

He seemed as wary as she was to cross that line
since she worked for him. Because James had a high
standard of ethics? Or was he simply unwilling to
jeopardize his child care arrangement? Maybe a

little of both. Either way, they'd been staying out of one another's way, never spending much time in each other's presence.

Now, decorating the playroom for Christmas, Lydia hummed a carol while the toddler raced in circles, tugging a Santa sleigh pull toy behind him. She liked reading to him before he fell asleep, but some nights he was simply too wound up to sit still. He liked running, jumping and climbing stairs, although she was always careful to follow him up each step, in case he fell. But he was agile and co-ordinated, just very energetic.

She angled back to look at the snowflake cling-on stickers she'd pressed to the playroom windows.

A quick knock sounded on the door before it opened.

She turned in time to see James lean into the room. It wasn't fair how quickly her belly filled with butterflies when she was around him.

"May I come in?" he asked, still dressed in his work clothes, jeans and a tee with the Double H logo.

He must have left his boots and hat in the mud-room, but she guessed he'd been working on one of the fences in a northern pasture. She'd seen him repairing it earlier in the week, too, when she'd taken Teddy out for a stroller ride along one of the better dirt roads on the ranch. She'd hoped James would take some time away from the chore to visit with his nephew, but he'd barely given them a wave before returning to the task.

She'd noticed that he kept long hours, and sometimes he didn't return to the house until well past nightfall. Could he possibly be as wary of time alone with her as she was of the forbidden temptation of his presence? Or could that just be her imagination? The man might truly be just a workaholic.

"Please do. I'm sure Teddy misses you. I've been hoping you could spend some more time with him." Lydia waved James in as she climbed down the step stool. "I only had the door closed so he didn't run out of the room."

She'd placed baby safety covers in the interior door knobs in the nursery and playroom to ensure the boy didn't wander out without her knowing.

"I won't stay long," James assured her, his dark eyes lingering on her. "It must be nearing the little guy's bedtime, right?"

A shiver of awareness snaked up her spine, and she thought about how she looked with her hair falling out of its ponytail and juice stains on her shirt. She almost reached to smooth her hair, then stopped herself for making the telling motion. Instead, she pulled her gaze away from her boss's enticing stare, focusing on Teddy.

"I'm not sure there's any sense putting him in his crib just yet. Look at him." Now that she had a rhythm to the days with the little boy, she knew it was time to get James more involved with him.

To help him feel more comfortable in his new role as the boy's father figure. There was more to being a good nanny than feeding and caring for a child. Part of the job was enabling a thriving family. And so far, she hadn't seen much emotional commitment from James, let alone one-on-one time with the boy.

"He looks like he's ready to run a marathon," James observed, patting the child's fluffy dark curls as Teddy rushed past him on wobbly legs.

"Exactly." Lydia noticed Teddy had dropped the pull string to the sleigh, though, his pattern of circling more erratic now. "And I've noticed when I force the bedtime issue, he only protests loudly, whereas if I wait an extra half hour, he usually settles down faster on his own."

"Mrs. Davis says you're doing an excellent job." James stepped deeper into the room, glancing toward the bag full of holiday decorations.

Her pulse skittered faster as he approached her.

"Really?" Lydia frowned. "I find that a little hard to imagine after all the times your housekeeper has glowered at me in the past two weeks."

"I'm sorry if she's made you uncomfortable. I will speak to her," he offered, taking a seat on the cushioned bench in front of a rocking chair.

"No. I didn't mean to suggest—" She definitely

didn't want to stir up trouble in the household. "She hasn't done anything to make me uncomfortable. And I'm glad to know she thinks I'm doing a good job."

Regretting the unguarded comment, she busied herself by reaching into her shopping bag to retrieve a quilted advent calendar. Farm animals peered out of the stitched barn, a new animal revealed each day until Christmas when a baby in a manger appeared in the center. She hung it from one of the plastic hooks meant to display a child's artwork.

When she turned around from her task, James had a smile on his face as he pointed to the playroom floor. Her gaze followed where he pointed to see Teddy lying on his side, a soft puppy dog rattle in one hand. Absently, the boy rubbed his fingers over the pale blue terry cloth, stroking the toy puppy's ear.

"Someone's getting sleepy." James spoke quietly. "Would you like me to carry him to his crib?"

"That would be great." Because while it was no trouble to lift him herself, Lydia had been wanting to get James more involved in the baby's daily routine. She watched as the rugged rancher leaned down to scoop up the child and cradle him against one big, broad shoulder.

James's shadowed jaw rested briefly atop his nephew's dark curls and Lydia's heart melted a little. Or maybe it was the sight of such a strong man displaying infinite tenderness toward a baby. No matter what it was that made her all soft and swoony inside, she recognized that standing shoulder to shoulder with her attractive employer in a darkened room might not be wise.

Lydia backed up a step as James headed down the hallway. "I'll be in the nursery in a minute," she assured him before darting in the other direction.

Just for a second, so she could get a handle on herself.

Instead of finding some breathing room, however, she stepped right into Mrs. Davis.

"Oh!" Lydia reached to right herself, placing a steadying hand against the wall. "I'm so sorry."

The housekeeper scowled, shaking her head. Her gray hair was down for the night, instead of in the tight twist she wore most days. Lydia was surprised to see her upstairs since she was usually in her room for the night at this hour. She tried not to react to the woman's displeased expression, remembering what James had said about the compliment she'd paid Lydia.

"I thought I heard Mr. Harris's voice," Mrs. Davis said. "I hoped to speak with him about something." The woman still wore the gray dress and apron that were her work uniform even though it was long past dinnertime.

"He's tucking Teddy into bed for the night."

Nodding, the housekeeper started to move toward the stairs and then turned back to Lydia.

"He is still grieving his brother, you know," Mrs. Davis said haltingly as she glanced toward the door to the nursery.

It was the most the housekeeper had ever said to her apart from where their duties overlapped.

"I'm sure he is," Lydia agreed. "It's only been a few months."

"And before that, he was dealing with the loss of his wife." Mrs. Davis lowered her voice even more while Lydia tried to conceal her shock.

James had been *married*?

She wanted to ask about that, but Mrs. Davis continued in her low, confidential tone. "I'm not sure he could handle getting attached to this boy and then possibly lose his nephew to the boy's grandparents. That's why I lobbied for Teddy to live with his grandparents from the start. I'm not heartless, Ms. Walker. I just don't want to see Mr. Harris hurt again."

Lydia could scarcely process all that, still reeling from the news that James had lost his wife. Had something happened to her? Had they divorced?

Before she could ask, James emerged from the nursery. Seeing the two women there, he paused.

Lydia was still too surprised to speak. Mrs. Davis straightened, and informed him, "The outdoor chest freezer needs to be replaced as soon as possible."

The two of them spoke briefly about that before resolving it to the housekeeper's satisfaction. Lydia told herself to simply say good-night and retreat.

Her boss's private affairs weren't her concern. Except what if his wife's family could make some kind of claim on Teddy? She knew that was a stretch considering the boy was James's blood relative. But still, wouldn't that have some bearing on her job? Or was she justifying her curiosity?

Before she could debate the wisdom of it, she blurted, "I didn't know you'd been married."

James braced for the inevitable pain that came from any reminder of his failed marriage.

To his surprise, it didn't come. Some resentment lingered, but not to the same degree. Had he finally put some of his past to rest? Because instead of feeling the old flare of anger about Raelynn, James only felt a surge of male satisfaction that Lydia Walker wanted to know about his romantic history.

"I didn't think it was relevant," he told her honestly. "I believe you've been as careful as I have about not getting too…personal."

He'd been working ridiculously long hours lately, not just to catch up with chores around the ranch, but to keep his distance from Lydia and their undeniable attraction. To avoid the intimacy of time together after that rainy night when he'd driven her to her house.

"It's none of my business, of course," she agreed, picking at a loose thread on the ribbed cuff of her pale green sweater sleeve.

A shade that brought out the green in her beautiful hazel eyes.

"It *is* your business. You work with my nephew, and my family status is relative to Teddy's." He gestured toward the stairs. "Let's talk in the kitchen and we can grab something to drink."

She followed him into the expansive kitchen, sliding onto one of the back-less saddle-shaped stools that pulled up to a long limestone countertop on an island. He tugged open one of the double doors to the refrigerator and chose two bottles of sparkling water and an orange. He sliced it and served a section on the rim of her glass along with her bottle.

"Thank you." She twisted off the cap and poured her own glass while he assembled some cheeses on a serving platter with a fresh baguette he found in the bread drawer.

Sliding onto the stool near her—carefully leaving a seat empty between them—he poured his own drink. The small pendant lights over the bar were on the nighttime setting, low enough to see what they were doing, but dim enough to be re-

laxing. He liked taking his meals here at the end
of a day.

"I don't talk about my ex-wife very often since
the divorce is just over a year old, and until recently,
it was a source of tremendous regret."

"You certainly don't owe me any explanations."
She slid a single slice of bread onto the appetizer
plate along with one slice of cheese. "I just wouldn't
want to be caught off guard if she came to the
house, or asked to see Teddy."

"That will never happen." For so many reasons.
"Raelynn never wanted children, for one thing."
He'd thought about that many times since bringing
his nephew into his life. If his wife hadn't left him
then, she sure as hell would have bolted when she
found out James was the guardian to a pint-sized
tornado. "But more importantly, she's moved out
of state. With her new husband."

Lydia stared at him, wide-eyed. "I'm so sorry."

"I'm not. At least we're not forced to see each
other around town." He'd been hurt at first when
he'd discovered how quickly she found someone
new, but even he'd been able to see that she was
happier in her second marriage. "I knew we were
having problems, but I didn't realize how much
she disliked being a rancher's wife. We agreed on
a settlement, and she left. End of story."

"That still must have been painful."

"Of course. But I learned a valuable lesson. Because while I don't plan to get hitched again, I do know that I'd take a more mercenary approach next time." He dragged the cutting board closer and cut the remainder of the orange he'd used for their drinks, adding the slices to the serving platter.

The sharp tang of citrus filled the air and Lydia helped herself to a segment.

"A mercenary approach to marriage?" She lifted an eyebrow. "That just sounds wrong."

"Think about how many more successful marriages there used to be when families helped arrange the match. A wedding was for practical purposes, yes. But when a partner shares your values and interests, love can grow out of that." His gaze snagged on the sheen of juice coating her lips, and he felt a new kind of thirst.

"You can't be serious." She shook her head, a smile tugging at the corners of her lips.

She mesmerized him so much it took him a moment to remember what they'd been talking about.

"I'm totally serious. I've given it a lot of thought, and I think maybe romance is overrated."

Picking up the slice of baguette on her plate, she tore it in half and pointed at him with the ripped half. "That much we can agree on."

"Oh really?" he asked while she took a bite. "I would hate to think that you're already a cynic when it comes to love, too." He was teasing her, but he felt sad to hear it. "I hope no one's trounced your heart, Lydia."

He'd seen her tenderness with Teddy, and it made him feel protective of her.

"No. But I know not everyone views marriage as a binding agreement." She slanted a glance his way. "My mother, for example, has taken a 'trial and error' approach to finding the right guy. She was married three times before I moved out of Arkansas, and she's contemplating husband number four even now."

"That couldn't have been easy for you or your siblings." He'd read about the family on the *House Rules* blog, but didn't remember anything about a father figure in the clan.

"We managed." There was a defensive note in her voice, a hint of defiant pride. "But it certainly gave me a skeptical view of matrimony."

He wondered if that meant she'd ruled it out for herself, but wasn't sure how much to push. He was curious, though.

"What about your dad?" he asked instead, wanting to know more about her. Because even though he'd been avoiding her for the last two weeks, that didn't mean he hadn't been thinking about her most waking hours. And fantasizing about her the second his head hit the pillow at night. "Did he remarry?"

"He did." She nodded, and then took a long sip

of her water. "My father is Brazilian, and he met my mother while he was a foreign exchange student. He went back home after things fell apart with my mother. I've only seen him once since then, and I've never met his second wife."

He wondered about her last name—Walker didn't strike him as Brazilian—but maybe she'd taken her mother's surname. When he didn't respond right away, Lydia smothered a laugh, stirring her orange around her glass with a cocktail straw.

"My family has some interesting dynamics, I realize."

"Every family is unique." He understood that. "My nephew will be faced with that challenge, too. Whether I keep him with me or his maternal grandparents raise him, his childhood will be very different from what it should have been."

Lydia was quiet for a long moment. "You're seriously considering…giving him up?"

"I'm hardly equipped to raise a child by myself." Frustration simmered, not that she'd raised the question, but because he hated the situation. Hated that his brother wasn't here to be the father he'd always dreamed of being. "I want what's best for the boy."

He reached for more food, filling his plate a second time. Busying himself to dodge a sense of crushing guilt.

"That's admirable to put his needs first," she said softly, reaching a hand over to touch his forearm. Distracting him from the mixture of unhappy emotions with that spike of awareness never far beneath the surface when she was near. "But if you really want what's best for Teddy, please don't rule yourself out yet. You might make a better father than you realize."

He knew the only reason he didn't discount the suggestion immediately was because of that gentle touch on his forearm. The cool brush of her skin along his. It made it impossible to think about anything else but her. His heart slugged hard against his ribs. His gaze dipped to her lips as they parted ever so slightly.

An invitation?

Or wishful imagining?

If she'd been closer, he would have kissed her. He couldn't decide, then, if it was good thing or a bad thing that there was a vacant seat between them, keeping them apart. Instead, he covered her hand with his, watching her all the while.

Her pupils widened a fraction. Even in the dim light of the kitchen, he could see that hint of reaction. A sign of shared desire.

She didn't pull away. At least, not at first.

After a moment, she blinked fast and then withdrew her fingers slowly.

"I'd better say good-night." She rose awkwardly

and backed toward the door before she turned away, her ponytail swishing as he watched her retreat.

He employed all his restraint not to follow her. Because he knew if he stood now, even just to extend their conversation, that kiss he wanted would somehow happen. It was so close he could almost taste her on his lips. And if this was what it was like between them after he'd deliberately avoided her for two weeks, what would happen if he spent more time with her and Teddy, the way she wanted him to?

He didn't have a plan for how to handle the magnetic attraction he felt for this woman, and he needed to come up with one. Fast. Because hiding out on the ranch, burying himself in physical labor, clearly wasn't working.

Five

Rose Clayton peered out her bedroom window just after dawn, not surprised to see James Harris's truck in one of the few remaining fields around the Silver C that didn't border Lone Wolf Ranch property. The Double H owner was a hard worker, no doubt, but over the past two weeks Rose had noticed James's truck at all hours in that shared pasture. The man was putting a lot of time into his place.

But then, she'd heard that his brother had died this past fall. Maybe James needed the distraction of exhausting, physical labor. She understood all too well the way grief could consume a person.

She'd grieved for the love she'd lost with Gus when her father had forced her to wed Edward. She'd grieved for her mother to be married to a man who didn't care about her. Eventually, she'd even hurt for her children, who'd been raised by a hard, unforgiving man.

Rose understood the way hard work could make a person forget, for a little while at least.

Turning from the window, she took a moment to inhale the scent of bacon frying in her kitchen. For the forty years she'd been married, she'd never once awoken to the scent of breakfast being made in her kitchen. All those years wed to Ed, she'd been the one doing the cooking since he'd never managed the ranch well enough to afford much help. At least, not for her.

Pulling on a pair of old jeans and a T-shirt from a recent rodeo, Rose took her time brushing her teeth, liking the idea that she would walk into her kitchen to find Gus Slade making her breakfast.

After all they'd been through, all the ways they'd hurt each other over the years, who would have thought they could end up together? It almost seemed too good to be true. Like if she pinched herself she might roll over in her bed and find it had all been a dream. Heaven knew, she'd dreamed of Gus often enough while married to the man handpicked by her daddy when she was only eighteen years old.

Now, running a brush through her short brown hair going gray at the temples, Rose breathed in the scent of fresh coffee and headed toward the kitchen. She tugged a soft blue sweater off the back of the bathroom door and tucked her arms into the sleeves, then padded out to the kitchen in sock feet.

Her overnight guest stood in front of the farmhouse sink, sipping from a red stoneware mug while the dawn light spilled through the window onto his thick white hair. Augustus "Gus" Slade had celebrated his sixty-ninth birthday this year, but he was still well muscled, strong enough to work the hay wagon if he was so inclined. And still undeniably sexy.

"Good morning." She couldn't help the smile that came with the words, the unexpected joy filling her whole body. It might not be the first time he'd spent the night with her, but it still felt magical to wake up to him.

Gus turned from the sink. "Good morning, beautiful." He toasted her with his coffee mug before setting it on the countertop. "Your breakfast is ready if you want to take a seat."

"I can help," she started, stepping toward the refrigerator to get the juice and creamer.

Gus made a shooing motion with his hand, chasing her toward the table. "I won't hear of it. I'm in charge of breakfast, so have a seat and get used to being spoiled."

"I will never get used to being spoiled," she admitted, wondering—not for the first time—what her life might have been like with this bold man at her side.

Would it have been this blissful every day? Or would she have been too young to appreciate how truly fortunate she was to have such a man? They'd been so in love as teens, until Gus went off to make his way in the world, promising to come back and marry her one day. Four years later he'd returned after earning enough money on the rodeo circuit to purchase a little piece of land nearby. Only her daddy was a cruel man who didn't want his daughter to have anything to do with a "nobody" like Gus. Jedediah Clayton had considered himself—and his daughter—too good for a Slade, forcing Rose to marry a man of Jed's choosing, threatening to kick out Rose's ill mother if Rose didn't do as he commanded.

She'd resented her father all her life for that. But now that Ed was long gone and Gus's wife, Sarah, had died, too, Rose wondered if she would have been as good of a wife to Gus as he deserved. He was an amazing man.

Stubborn. Surly. And one hell of a ranching rival all those years that they'd been bitterly estranged, with Gus blaming Rose for marrying another man. But that was all in the past. Gus now knew that Rose had married Ed only out of fear for her mother.

"Then you underestimate me, Rose Clayton," Gus promised, stepping closer to her so he could fold her hands in his. "Because you don't know what great lengths I would go to in order to spoil you."

That joy bubbled up inside her again, making her feel like a giddy teenager falling in love with him all over again.

"Gus, all of Royal thinks I'm the toughest old bird in the county." She had spent a lifetime reinforcing the defenses around her heart and her life, trying to focus on her family and the ranch instead of all that she'd given up. "What will they say if you turn me soft?"

Gus's piercing blue eyes seemed to peer right into her soul. "They may say I'm one hell of a lucky man to win over the hottest woman in town."

She laughed. "You're too much."

The look he gave her about melted her socks off, before he kissed her tenderly on the cheek.

"Then have a seat, Rose, and let me get your breakfast."

Before she could move away, a voice cleared on the far side of the room. Rose tensed, her cheeks heating to be "caught" by her grandson, Daniel, the ranch manager of the Silver C.

Tall and well built, Daniel had turned into a formidable man who made Rose so proud. She'd gladly raised him from boyhood when her own daughter had been overwhelmed by single parenthood, turning to alcohol instead of her family for help. Rose blamed Ed for that, but she hadn't given up hope on Stephanie.

"Good morning, Daniel." She waved him over to the table. "Join us for some breakfast."

Daniel scowled. "I'll take something for the road," he muttered, stepping into the pantry before coming out with a few protein bars. "And Gran, have you thought about what you're doing, carrying on like this with this man?"

Flustered to have her own grandchild call her out, Rose was at a loss for words, her cheeks heating even though she had no cause to be embarrassed.

"Your grandmother does not 'carry on,' son," Gus told him mildly as he slid slices of bacon onto two plates. "Show her some respect."

Rose's gaze darted to Daniel's. The younger man looked as uncomfortable as she felt. Although she did appreciate Gus's easy defense of her.

"I meant no disrespect," Daniel insisted, scrubbing a hand through his dark hair. "But Gran is a well-respected member of the community. People will start to talk when they see your truck here every night."

Would people talk? She hadn't thought about

that, but Daniel probably had a point. People did love gossip.

"That's no one's business but ours." Gus smiled at her as he strode closer to the table, her plate in hand. He set it in front of her while she took a seat. "But if it will put your mind at ease, I love your grandmother very much, and soon I'm going to marry her, like I should have all those years ago."

Is he serious? she thought wildly, her heart racing faster.

Her gaze went to Gus's, seeing the calm self-assurance in his blue eyes. Of course he was serious.

Just when she thought she couldn't feel any more joy in this life…boom. She felt a deep sense of happiness, as if the world was suddenly tilted right again. But she tucked those thoughts away for now, in front of Daniel, knowing her grandson didn't share her joy.

Not when his own heart was so thoroughly broken. Worse? She feared it was all her fault.

Lydia wasn't surprised when she awoke the next day to discover that James had left town on a business trip. He'd sent her a text with his contact information for a hotel in Houston in case she needed anything.

She didn't know much more than that, so throughout the week, she'd tried to look at his absence as a good thing—a favor that made her job easier. Without him in the house, she didn't have to worry about the attraction leading to anything. Except, as she went through the motions of her job, bringing Teddy for a holiday shopping outing and to have his photo taken with Santa, Lydia couldn't deny that she missed seeing her boss.

And in some ways, that felt even more dangerous to her peace of mind than the ever-present awareness between them. When he wasn't around, she found her subconscious supplied plenty of fantasy scenarios starring him.

Late in the week, shortly past dinnertime, she was in the kitchen storing some toddler portions of veggies that she'd cooked in batches for Teddy. The little boy still sat in his high chair, chasing oat cereal around his tray, tired out from the day since they'd skipped naptime while they were out doing errands.

Midway through the cooking operation, Lydia realized she'd gravitated toward the chore out of habit, an old way of coping with stress from the days when she'd lived under her mother's roof. Back then, she'd always found comfort in the ritual of work when her mother's love life got too crazy. Or her mother was too busy being romanced by her latest "Mr. Right" that she forgot to film a podcast for her blog. Lydia appreciated the way work made her feel in control.

And today, while she and Teddy had been out shopping, her mother had texted to remind her that

Fiona expected a spa day before her bachelorette party—both of which were Lydia's job to organize as her maid of honor. Clearly, her mom had ignored the fact that Lydia refused to be in the wedding.

Here she was two hours later, chopping carrots and butternut squash like a madwoman, all because she hadn't found a way to make her mother listen.

Lydia heard the doorbell ring, and she assumed Mrs. Davis answered it when she heard the low rumble of voices in the front of the house. They had visitors.

And one of the voices—a woman's—she felt sure she recognized.

"Do you want to see who's here?" she asked Teddy, already unbuckling the straps on the high chair so she could lift him up.

"See here," he repeated in perfect imitation of her.

It was the first time she'd heard that combination of words, far more complicated than *bye-bye* or *coo-kie*, both of which he used well.

"Yes!" The sound of his clear words cheered her, reminding her that her work here was so much more than a job. More than a means to repay her sister's debt. In so many ways her involvement with children was a gift. "That's right, Teddy. We're going to see who is here."

She settled him on her hip and he laid his head

against her shoulder. She couldn't resist resting her cheek on his fluffy crop of curls for a moment while she breathed in the scent of baby shampoo.

Then, she headed into the living area so she had a clear view of the foyer. She recognized Tessa Noble, a woman she'd gotten to know through her sister Gail, standing beside the tall, handsome rancher who'd bid on Tessa at the same charity bachelor auction where Gail had bid on Lloyd Richardson. Lydia recognized him only from photos in the articles she'd read online about the auction.

"Hello, Tessa." She strode closer to greet the woman who'd been supportive of Gail's fledgling grocery delivery business. Now, in simple heeled boots and jeans with her blue hoodie and a bright orange scarf, Tessa wore her dark hair loose and curly, but there was something about her that just glowed. "I don't know if you remember me—"

"Of course I do, Lydia." Tessa gave her a wide smile, stepping deeper into the room, her light brown eyes darting over the child in Lydia's arms. "But I sure didn't expect to see you here."

Before Lydia could reply, Mrs. Davis excused herself to retreat downstairs for the evening, leaving the guests to her.

Lydia waved the couple into the room. "Would you like to have a seat? James is away on business, but you're more than welcome—"

"We won't stay." Tessa exchanged a quick look

with her tall, green-eyed companion. "This is Ryan Bateman, by the way. Ryan, Lydia Walker is Gail's older sister."

Lydia shook the man's hand and he gave her a warm smile.

"We just came by to thank James for encouraging Tessa to take part in the bachelor auction." He slid his arm around Tessa's waist, tucking her close as if he'd missed her in the brief moment they hadn't been side by side. "Tessa's been my best friend for a long time, but without the nudge of that night, I don't know how long it would have taken me to see that she was the right woman for me all along."

Tessa, who already glowed with happiness, brightened even more as she flashed a stunning ring on her left finger—chocolate and white diamonds set in a rose gold band. "I couldn't wait to tell James that we're getting married."

The new couple's love warmed the whole room. And while Lydia was thrilled for them, it was hard not to feel like a romantic failure by comparison.

"That's wonderful news! Tessa, your ring is gorgeous." She wished Gail was here to share her friend's engagement news. "I'm so happy for you and I know James will be thrilled for you, too." Unwilling to linger on the topic of the charity auction since she hadn't worked out what to say about her sister's exorbitant bid, Lydia steered the conversation away from the event. "I'm working here as Teddy's nanny, by the way, so I'm sure to see James as soon as he returns."

Not that she had any idea when that might be.

With Christmas just a few days away, she wondered if he would stay away for the holiday. What if her presence in the house was actually preventing him from bonding with his nephew? The thought made hear heart ache for the boy.

Tessa ducked to peer into Teddy's face. "He's almost asleep. He looks very comfortable with you, Lydia, but please let James know that I'd be happy to help out with the baby on your days off."

"That's very kind of you. Thank you." She'd thought about taking Teddy with her the next time she had a meeting with her contractor if James hadn't returned to town by then, but it was nice to know Tessa didn't mind the occasional babysitting gig. "James worries that Teddy can be a handful, but I think it's just because he's been through so much these last few months."

"Poor baby." Tessa stroked the boy's back for a moment, her face softening. "He needs his uncle now more than ever."

The woman's words were a powerful reminder of what Lydia had thought all along.

If she wanted to be a good nanny to Teddy, she needed to recommit to bringing James more firmly into the child's routine. A task that wasn't easy if James continued to keep his distance.

So while Lydia said good-night to the guests, waving at them while they headed out to Ryan's big black pickup truck in the driveway, Lydia was already formulating a plan to bring James home for good. No matter that his presence was an undeniable temptation for her. The sweet child in her arms deserved to know the comfort of a father figure.

James sat in a luxury hotel suite in Houston, working on taxes three days before Christmas.

He couldn't decide if he felt like Scrooge for working with figures when the rest of the world was preparing for the holiday, or if should feel proud of himself for starting the Double H's tax forms before the year ended. Either way, the kind of jump start was a first for him and he owed it all to the woman who'd dominated his thoughts all week.

Lydia.

The phone rang even as he thought her name, the screen showing her as the incoming call. Not really a coincidence given that he'd been thinking of her more often than not.

He checked the antique timepiece that had belonged to his grandfather. A trickle of anxiety made him wonder if everything was okay back home when he saw it was almost nine o'clock.

"Hello, Lydia." He wished he could see her face. Know her expression right now.

"Hi." She didn't sound upset. Somehow, through that one syllable, he could tell by her tone that there was nothing wrong with his nephew. "How's Houston?"

Relief kicked through him hard, making him realize how attached he was growing to the boy in spite of himself. Pushing away from the hotel room's small desk, he tipped back in the rolling chair to peer out his window at the city skyline.

"It's quiet. I've been taking meetings with some locals who are interested in expanding the Texas Cattleman's Club into Houston, but I could wrap things up anytime now." He needed to be back in Royal, in fact, and had extended the trip this long only to make sure he gave Lydia space to get comfortable in his home.

He didn't want to crowd her with the heat that seemed inevitable when they were in the same room.

"That's good," she said in a rush. "I was calling to see if you could spend some time with Teddy this weekend."

Frowning, he straightened in the leather desk chair.

"Do you need time off?" He hadn't thought about what to do if Lydia wanted some downtime.

But he recognized that her work made her on-call twenty-four hours a day.

"No. I'd be here, too," she clarified. "I just thought it would be nice for Teddy if you could spend some time with him." She seemed to hesitate a moment, before adding, "And he seems to be settling into a routine, which I think is helping with some of the behavior issues he might have had before. He's fun to be around."

James felt like a heel. Did she think that's why he'd been staying away? Because of a tantrum or two? Worse, what if she had a point? He'd been so quick to give over complete care of the child to her. And no matter what he thought about his brother's decision to appoint James as Teddy's legal guardian, he owed his brother better than paying lip service to Parker's wishes. Frustration simmered, and he rose to his feet, pacing the hotel suite.

Even if Teddy eventually went to live with his grandparents, James always wanted him to feel welcome at the Double H.

"I will be home tomorrow," he assured her, mentally making room in his schedule. "How do you suggest we spend the day?"

"Oh. Um…thank you." She sounded surprised. And pleased. "In that case, there's a holiday ice show that he might enjoy. Even if we only get to see a part of it, I think it would be fun for him."

"Of course. I'll take care of the tickets tonight.

Should we do anything else? Dinner afterward?" He couldn't deny that he was looking forward to spending time with Lydia.

"We might be pushing our luck with an active toddler," she mused aloud. "What if we bring him out to get a Christmas tree?"

"Even though we already have one?" He'd sent one of the ranch hands to the house last week to help Mrs. Davis take one out of storage.

There was a pause on the other end of the call.

"You don't like my Christmas tree?" he pressed, trying to remember what it looked like.

"It's beautiful." She seemed to be weighing her words. "But maybe we could cut down a little one for the playroom where Teddy and I could hang some homemade ornaments? You know, give him a little more buy-in?"

James couldn't help but laugh.

"By all means, a kid should have buy-in on his own Christmas." Yet even as he spoke the words, he realized there wasn't a damned thing funny about it. If anything, he found it sad to think of his nephew not being a part of a family Christmas.

The sudden punch of grief hit hard while Lydia suggested a playroom picnic afterward.

Only half listening, he was lost in his own thoughts for a moment as James recognized that he'd been screwing up his time with Teddy. He'd been so focused on providing the boy with better care than he could offer him personally, he'd ended up having very little to do with the child. His last remaining relative.

And he had Lydia to thank for helping him to see that before Teddy's grandparents got involved. He still had time to make memories with the boy. Ensure that he felt at home in the house where his father was raised.

"That all sounds good," James told her before she signed off for the night. "I've been trying to give you space. To make things easier for you while you get settled at the ranch." He hesitated. Did he need to spell out his reasons? He was pretty sure she knew all about the crackle of awareness between them. "But I'm definitely ready to spend more time with you and Teddy."

"I know Teddy will be happy to have you back home," she admitted softly, as careful as ever with her words.

His last question remained unspoken.

Would *she* be happy to have him back in the house with her every day? Every *night*?

This would be the last time he backed off that question, however. Tomorrow, they were going to face their simmering mutual attraction head-on and see what happened. No more letting it keep him from his nephew. Decision made, he felt a surge of anticipation.

"Good," he said simply. "I'm looking forward to

seeing him, and *you*, too. Very much." He let the words hover there for a moment, wanting them to linger in her mind long after the call disconnected. "Sleep well, Lydia."

Morning couldn't come soon enough.

Six

Seated beside James in a black BMW sedan the next day, Lydia reminded herself not to think about his phone call the night before. The one where he'd said how much he was looking forward to seeing her.

After all, she'd already lost sleep thinking about what he'd meant. She didn't dare lose focus on her job now that he was back in Royal, bringing her and Teddy on the special outing she'd requested.

Still, as the sleek luxury car sped toward the civic center for the holiday ice show, she couldn't help thinking how much the trip felt like a date. Especially with Teddy quietly taking in the scen-

ery from his car seat. There was no need to enter-
tain the baby with silly songs or toys passed over
her shoulder. There was only the scent of leather
seats and a hint of spicy aftershave. The sound of
steel guitars muted from the speakers. And the too-
rapid beat of her heart as she smoothed the belted
trench coat over her knees to cover the hem of her
red sweater dress.

She was hyperaware of the compelling man behind the wheel. He wore black pants and a dark
polo shirt with a camel-colored blazer and suede
boots. Well dressed but not overdressed for an ice
show meant for families. The tailored jacket accen-
tuated his lean, muscular physique. No doubt she
was gawking a little as he navigated easily through
midday traffic for the matinee show.

Searching for a topic to distract her, she remembered the visitors from the night before.

"I'm not sure if Mrs. Davis mentioned it, but
Tessa Noble and Ryan Bateman stopped in yesterday evening to thank you for encouraging Tessa to
go on the auction block at the Pancreatic Cancer
Research Foundation event." She remembered how
starry-eyed they both looked. How glowing with
happiness. "They are engaged to be married, and
very much in love."

"Is that right?" James grinned as he glanced
over at her. "And Tessa was always his best friend

before." The deep timbre of his voice hummed right through her.

"Ryan said the auction was the nudge he needed to see her in a different light."

"I couldn't be happier for them." He frowned. "Although the last I knew, Rose Clayton was angling for her grandson, Daniel, to date Tessa."

Lydia recalled the matriarch of the Silver C only from the occasional sightings around Royal and the woman's charitable efforts in town. Everyone seemed to know about the enmity between the Claytons and the Slades, Royal's answer to the Hatfields and McCoys. As a newcomer to town, Lydia had heard only bits of gossip about old battles over property lines and water rights. The feud might be dying down now that Rose Clayton's husband was long gone and Gus Slade's wife, Sarah, had passed away. The Great Royal Bachelor Auction had been dedicated to the memory of Sarah Slade, in fact.

"Well, Tessa is most definitely taken," Lydia observed. "Rose will have to turn her matchmaking efforts elsewhere."

"After the press coverage Daniel received following the auction, he shouldn't have any trouble finding his own dates. The story calling him the 'Most Eligible Bachelor in Texas' was picked up all over the place." James pulled off the interstate onto the ramp that led toward the civic center.

Colorful billboards hung outside the arena with ads for upcoming shows, including one for the holiday ice show.

"Look, Teddy." Lydia pointed to the characters twirling on skates. "Do you see the polar bear?"

He clapped his hands once, his brown eyes wide with childish wonder. She adored this little boy.

"Bear," he said.

Clear as a bell. She couldn't help a swell of pride in him.

"Wow. Did you teach him that?" James sounded as awed as his nephew.

She flushed with pleasure, even if she couldn't take credit.

"No. Kids his age are little sponges, soaking it all in. He surprised me yesterday by repeating a phrase really clearly."

"That's incredible." He drummed his thumbs on the steering wheel while he waited for a parking space. The lot was already busy. While he waited, he glanced over at her, his gaze lingering. "And it's easy to see you've been a good influence on him. He seems calmer."

She knew the praise shouldn't feel any different from the approval she'd received from other satisfied parents in the past. Yet somehow, coming from this handsome, charismatic man, it meant more. Or maybe she just wanted more with him. The realization—that it wasn't just physical attraction between them but maybe something deeper—rattled her.

She was growing attached to James and his sweet nephew.

"Thank you," she said thickly, dragging her gaze away from his. "We've had fun together." Then, in a rush, she added, "Teddy and I."

Her cheeks felt warm. All of her felt warm from his attention. His praise. This damned awareness.

"And I appreciate you helping me to be a part of that," he said smoothly as he parked the sedan and switched off the ignition. In the quiet aftermath, he slid his hand over hers where it rested on the console. "No matter what else happens between us, Lydia, with your job or our agreement, please know that I am deeply grateful to you for stepping in to help me with my nephew. I realized last night that I was screwing up the one thing my brother asked of me."

Behind them in the backseat, Teddy made cooing sounds as he kicked the base of his car seat with one sneaker. The boy was content.

And she was completely caught off guard by James's sincerity. Not to mention his touch. She wondered if her racing heart was obvious where his finger lay along her forearm. Her breath caught as she went to answer.

"I'm glad I could help." She told herself if he

moved his hand away now, then the touch was just an indication of simple human gratitude.

His hand remained.

"The last thing I want to do is complicate matters between us when you're so good for Teddy." His thumb shifted along her inner arm. Just a fraction of an inch. A tiny stroke of her wrist. Back and forth. "But I can't be with you and pretend that I don't feel drawn to you. Because I do, Lydia. That's the reason I spent this past week in Houston. And why I worked all the long hours on the ranch before I left. I tried my best to stay away."

She was spellbound by his touch. Gentle, but sure. She had no doubt he would remove his hand instantly if she asked him to. She met his eyes again, shifting toward him to meet his gaze head-on, his words sinking in.

"Because of me," she clarified, surprised that he would admit it so plainly.

There would be no taking back these words. No pretending this conversation hadn't happened. And where did that leave them, now that their mutual attraction was out there in the open? A tangible thing they couldn't hide from, especially while living under the same roof.

"Because I didn't want you to feel uncomfortable." He slid his hand under hers and then laid his other palm on top, capturing her fingers between his. "But I realized last night when you called that staying away from you wasn't good for Teddy. And I'm not interested in staying apart from you either, even if it means that we have to revisit our arrangement."

"But we only just worked out the details of how I can help Gail repay you." She opted to focus on that last part of what he'd said—about revisiting their arrangement—since she wasn't ready to think about why he wanted to renegotiate the agreement. "I don't know if I trust Gail to make an honest effort to repay you in some way, and I can't just let it go either."

"I don't want you to quit, Lydia. Just the opposite, in fact. But I guess, right now, all I really want to know is this." He stared down at the place where their hands were joined, studying the knot of fingers like a complex problem before he looked up at her again. "Could we not worry about our professional relationship so that, just for today, I could kiss you the way I've wanted to for weeks?"

They were already so close. That kiss was just a breath away, but indulging in it meant admitting that she wanted it, too. And while James had clearly already come to terms with confronting this desire, Lydia hadn't wrapped her brain around all the ways a relationship could complicate things.

Desire tightened inside her, the need for him turning into an ache.

"I wish it was that simple." She whispered her thoughts aloud, unable to move away from him.

"Do you?" He raked his gaze over her and she felt the heat of his longing as thoroughly as her own.

Her skin tingled, and it was all she could do to nod. Yes. She craved that kiss.

"Then that will have to be enough. For now." Sliding his hands away from hers, he lifted a finger to skim along her cheek. Then dragged his thumb along her lower lip in a way that did something sweetly erotic to her insides. "Knowing that you're thinking about that kiss, too..." He let the thought trail off along with his touch before he leaned back in his seat. "That's more than I had at the beginning of this day. And that's a start."

He was out of the vehicle and around to her side of the car, opening the door for her before she caught her breath. With a stern warning to herself to rein it in, Lydia redoubled her focus on Teddy. On making this a memorable day for the little boy who deserved a happy Christmas outing.

But she'd be lying if she said she wasn't thinking about kissing James, too. Every. Single. Moment.

That evening, after the holiday ice show and the trip to cut down a small Christmas tree for the playroom, James sat with legs sprawled on the red-and-green tartan picnic blanket. It was only eight o'clock, but time spent with a toddler made it feel later. Teddy had been well behaved all day. His exclamations at the ice show were no louder than the majority of the crowd made up of almost 50 percent kids. The toddler had grown weary of sitting in the seat after about forty-five minutes, so they'd slipped out during a change of scenery and brought him out on a sleigh to hike around the ranch and choose a little three-foot tree that was perfect for the play area.

They'd decorated it with only a couple of snow-flakes that Lydia had made ahead of time, but she'd said they would add to it in the coming days. Besides, Teddy had set some of his toys on the branches. The rubber balls hadn't worked out as ornaments, but a couple of his stuffed toys and a few blocks still rested on the boughs. No surprise that Lydia had been correct about the boy needing a more hands-on tree. Teddy still sat on the floor beside it, now dressed in his pajamas while Lydia read a story to him from a plastic-coated book.

She glanced toward James as she read, and any sense of contentment with the day fled like smoke from a fire. Just that one shared look and his mind rewound to the intriguing conversation they'd had in the parking lot before the ice show.

When he'd been a moment away from kissing her. He studied her now, as her attention returned to the baby and his book. With her boots off, he could see her polka-dot Christmas socks. Gold hoop earrings shone in the lamplight with her light brown hair twisted into a low braid.

Realizing how close they were to Teddy's bedtime, and the hour he would finally have Lydia all to himself, James made quick work of the picnic remains. He packed the few containers of leftover fruit and cheeses back into the straw basket that the cook had delivered earlier in the day. Then, he rolled up the blanket carefully and tucked it under the basket's handle.

"How about I tuck him in?" he offered, wanting to show Lydia he'd heard her concerns about spending more time with his nephew.

He wanted the boy to always feel welcome here, even if Teddy's maternal grandparents decided they were ready to raise him.

"That would be great. Thank you." She closed the book and rose. "I'll bring the picnic hamper to the kitchen."

He lifted Teddy in his arms.

"The maid will get it." He had a cleaning service twice a week to help Mrs. Davis. "Why don't you head to the library and I'll meet you down there? I have a surprise for you."

"A surprise?" She leaned closer so she could ruffle Teddy's hair.

The soft vanilla scent of her lingered after she eased away. Hunger for her stirred.

"It will only take a minute. I know you've had a full day with this guy." He lifted Teddy slightly and the boy giggled. "I'll see you in a few."

Turning on his heel, he went to lay Teddy in his crib. It had gone well enough the last time he'd done it that he felt more sure of himself this time. Besides, the kid had to be tired after how busy they'd kept him all day long.

Flicking on the night-light and the nursery monitor, James made sure the crib was clear of extra toys. He was old enough for a light blanket and a stuffed rattle, but the baby seemed content to poke one foot through the slats of the crib, making babbling sounds.

Right up until he said, "Night-night."

The words clutched at James's heart, making him glad again that he'd come back to Royal today. He might not be ready for kids of his own, but he didn't want to screw up this window of time with his nephew. Not when Parker had entrusted him to care for the boy.

"Good night, Teddy," he called back to him, before shutting the door.

He carried the receiver for the baby monitor downstairs with him, his thoughts turning to the alluring woman who waited for him in his library. He hadn't dated anyone seriously since his divorce, going out a few times just to prove to himself he could.

Now? Lydia dominated his thoughts, and not just because she was good with Teddy.

She was honorable, for one thing. She hadn't needed to seek him out after her sister fled town without paying for her bachelor. But here Lydia was, trying to salvage the integrity of her family name. Doing what she thought was right.

She worked hard, for another, taking her job seriously. The difference she'd already made with Teddy was all the proof he needed.

And, as he stepped through the open library doors to see her silhouetted by moonlight streaming through the windows of an otherwise darkened room, James was reminded how incredibly sexy she was, too. The sweater dress hugged her curves, her face tipped upward. She'd slipped into the leather boots she'd worn earlier in the day, the heels making her almost as tall as him.

"You should see the moon," she said softly. "It's so huge above the tree line, it looks like a movie set. Or a honky-tonk bar."

He sucked in a breath, steeling himself for the inevitable draw of her nearness. Knowing the next move had to be hers after he'd made his intentions clear this afternoon.

"One of the benefits of living out here," he admitted. "No city lights or buildings to get in the way of the view."

He stopped short of her, since touching her again was out of the question. Without the barrier of the baby around, he had only his own restraint to rely on. And he sure as hell wasn't going to test it for a second time today.

He leaned against the windowsill the same way she did, leaving two feet between them.

"Thank you for today." She folded her arms, one shoulder tipping against the glass pane. "For coming home and being a part of everything I had planned."

"I know you did it for Teddy." She'd been very clear about her motives. Very careful to draw boundaries. "But I had fun, too."

"So did I." Her hazel eyes locked on his.

Desire for her flared hotter. His hands itched to reach for her. To pull her against him and keep her there while he tested the softness of her lips. Tasted his fill.

Instead, he eased away from the window, needing more space from her if he was going to maintain this facade of a professional relationship. "Are you ready to see your surprise?"

Her eyebrow arched. Straightening, she nodded. "Absolutely."

"Then follow me." He headed toward the back wall of the library, to a door almost hidden by bookshelves. The room was designed that way, giving this added space an intimate ambiance. "I have a secret retreat that I thought you might enjoy some evenings after Teddy goes to bed."

He slid open the door with the antique brass handle and hit the switch for the floor lights. Inside, tiny white bulbs glowed on either side of the aisle down the center of his media room. Big leather chairs flanked the aisle in pairs, for sixteen seats in all. The screen ahead was dark for a moment until he hit a command on his phone and cued up the opening credits of a nature documentary. On the screen, the sun rose on an African savannah while birds dipped and called. He hit the mute button but let the video run.

"All this time you've been hiding a home movie theater in here?" Her fingers smoothed along the leather seat rest of a chair. "What a great space."

"I didn't show it to you that first day because I had a few clients in to look at film of one of our horses in training and there was still some electronic equipment out." He rolled aside one of the screens on some built-in shelving to show her a sample of the technology not in use at the moment. "This isn't always a good spot for a toddler. But I thought you might enjoy unwinding here sometimes."

"I will. May I?" At his nod, she lowered herself into one of the chairs as if to test it out. "This is so comfortable. Do you ever fall asleep watching movies?"

He sat in the chair beside her, only an armrest separating them in the dim room while the film showed a family of lions on the move. "Never. Believe it or not, I've only used the room for previewing racing footage or rodeo competitions since our training program involves a lot of animal analysis."

Lydia made a face, wrinkling her nose. "You remember what they say about all work and no play?"

"Guilty." He couldn't deny it. Although being around this woman made him want to be someone different. Someone more inclined to have fun. "But my life has been anything but dull these last few weeks."

Leaning deeper into the seat back, she turned to look at him. She appeared comfortable. More relaxed than he'd ever seen her. Was she more at ease now that Teddy was sleeping? Or maybe she was simply worn out from a long day of caregiving.

"Mine, too." A smile hitched at her lips. "James, I haven't forgotten what we talked about in the car today."

Anticipation fired through him, but he didn't shift closer. Didn't touch her. He'd put the ball in her court for making the next move and he intended to be patient while she grappled with the hunger he'd wrestled since they first met. "It's been on my mind all day, too."

"I'm afraid I still don't have any more answers than I did earlier." Frowning, she nibbled at her lip for a moment as she turned her eyes toward the viewing screen where little lion cubs tackled each other. Then, she glanced back at him. "Although, I will say it's easier to contemplate a kiss when I'm not working."

The words reverberated through him like a bell, the hum of it remaining in his body long after she finished speaking. Every nerve ending acutely attuned to her.

He slid his hand under the armrest between them and tilted it up and out of the way. Removing the only physical barrier between them, but not crossing it.

"Then, solely in the interest of refreshing your memory, I'd like to remind you of my proposition."

Her shoulder angled a fraction closer to him. "Please do."

Her words were a throaty rasp of air as her fingers landed lightly on his chest.

She had to feel the rapid thrum of his heart. Wanting more.

"I thought we should shove aside all the things keeping us apart and just test run that kiss." He liked her hand on him, not just because it felt so damn good to have her touch him, but also because it freed him to touch her back.

He cradled her jaw in one hand, testing the softness of her lower lip with his thumb.

"See if it's worthwhile?" she asked.

The play of her mouth against his skin mesmerized him as she arched closer still.

"Something like that." He watched up until the last moment when her lips brushed his.

A tentative exploration. A minty breath. The tender grip of her fist twisting his shirt placket.

And then, confident he'd let her make the first move, he wrapped his arms around her, dragging her against him. She was so soft and sweetly scented, her hair fraying loose from its confining braid and her sweater dress teasing his skin.

He molded her curves to the hard planes of his body, liking the way she fit against him. Needing more, but knowing it wasn't time yet.

Knowing he'd negotiated for only a kiss. A taste.

He focused on just that—the feel of her lips and the damp stroke of her tongue. He gave and took in equal measures, exploring what she liked, breathing her in. Her hands were restless on him, gliding up his arms and down his chest.

Her touch made it impossible to pull away. She felt so damned good in his arms. So right. He adjusted the angle, deepening the kiss, telling himself it was just for a moment. She gripped his shoulders tightly, dragging him closer. Her breasts brushed his chest, and the contact made everything hotter, threatening his control.

He kissed her until his restraint stretched as thin as he dared.

Only then did he ease away carefully. Slowly.

Lydia's eyes fluttered open, her lips still parted. Damp.

With an effort, he closed his eyes. Let go of her completely.

"I should—um. Go." She sounded rattled. Or maybe she was simply as revved up as him.

But he couldn't have stopped her. Not without falling into that kiss all over again. So he just nodded tightly, remaining in his seat while she rose to her feet.

On the screen behind her, he saw night had fallen on the savannah. As for the test run of a kiss, he wasn't sure if he'd call it a success or a failure since it turned out to be the most combustible kiss he'd ever experienced.

One thing he knew for sure, though. He wouldn't try that again unless they were both prepared for it to lead to a whole lot more.

Seven

With Christmas just days away, Rose Clayton suspected she should have been prepared for the crowds of people at the Courtyard Shops just west of Royal's downtown area. This was the town's most popular shopping district, the property a reclaimed old farm where the big red barn was now an antiques store and the main house sheltered local artisans. But it had been so long since Rose had shopped for something in person—as opposed to online or through one of her ranch's administrative assistants—that she'd forgotten how much of a crush the holiday shopping outing could be. It seemed like she'd seen half the townspeople here in the last

"FAST FIVE" READER SURVEY

Your participation entitles you to:
* ✷ **4 Thank-You Gifts Worth Over $20!**

Complete the survey in minutes.

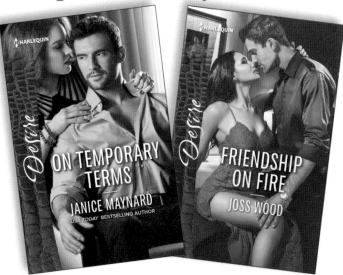

Get **2 FREE** Books

Your Thank-You Gifts include **2 FREE BOOKS** and **2 MYSTERY GIFTS**. There's no obligation to purchase anything!

See inside for details.

Dear Reader,

Since you are a lover of our books, your opinions are important to us... and so is your time.

That's why we made sure your **"FAST FIVE" READER SURVEY** can be completed in just a few minutes. Your answers to the five questions will help us remain at the forefront of women's fiction.

And, as a thank-you for participating, we'd like to send you **4 FREE THANK-YOU GIFTS!**

Enjoy your gifts with our appreciation,

Pam Powers

To get your
4 FREE THANK-YOU GIFTS:

✱ Quickly complete the "Fast Five" Reader Survey
and return the insert.

"FAST FIVE" READER SURVEY

1	Do you sometimes read a book a second or third time?	○ Yes ○ No
2	Do you often choose reading over other forms of entertainment such as television?	○ Yes ○ No
3	When you were a child, did someone regularly read aloud to you?	○ Yes ○ No
4	Do you sometimes take a book with you when you travel outside the home?	○ Yes ○ No
5	In addition to books, do you regularly read newspapers and magazines?	○ Yes ○ No

YES! I have completed the above Reader Survey. Please send me my 4 FREE GIFTS (gifts worth over $20 retail). I understand that I am under no obligation to buy anything, as explained on the back of this card.

225/326 HDL GM3T

FIRST NAME	LAST NAME

ADDRESS

APT.#	CITY

STATE/PROV.	ZIP/POSTAL CODE

hour, from local rancher Caleb Mackenzie and his fiancée, Shelby Arthur, to the newly engaged Ryan Bateman and Tessa Noble.

Then again, maybe Rose's eye was simply drawn to all the happy couples in town. She wanted that kind of happiness for her grandson, Daniel.

And for herself.

Taking a moment to rest in front of the live pine tree decorated with lights and oversize ornaments just outside the antiques shop, Rose soaked in the atmosphere. From the local children's choir singing carols to the scent of hot pretzels and roasted chestnuts, the outdoor venue oozed holiday cheer. Or maybe it was her who was filled with so much goodwill in the days following Gus's declaration that he was going to marry her.

Had he meant it?

Or had he just told Daniel that in an effort to keep the peace? She hadn't wanted to quiz Gus about it, unwilling to ripple the waters in this tenuous new joyful place in her life. Besides, daydreaming about a future with him made her feel like a teenager again.

Except this time, she began to think their story could have a happy ending.

"Hello, Rose." The deep timbre of a male voice sounded nearby, and she turned to see her neighbor, James Harris.

Dressed in dark jeans and a coffee-colored

suede jacket, he looked more relaxed than the last time she'd seen him—working tirelessly to restring fencing near her property line.

"Nice to see you, James." She hadn't attended his brother's funeral halfway across the state, but she'd sent flowers with her condolences. The Harris family had been good to her over the years and she was sorry to see James lose a brother at such a young age. "I've been wondering how you're doing with a toddler in the house."

"Hanging in there." He grinned as he tipped up his Stetson a fraction, juggling his shopping bags over to one hand. "I found a nanny who has really been making a difference with Teddy. Her name is Lydia Walker and I'm sure you'll see her around the ranch sooner or later."

"Mrs. Davis mentioned her to me when she came over to store some things in our extra freezer." Rose gathered the older woman wasn't thrilled with the new hire, but then Bernadette Davis had always been protective of the Harris boys. She'd been livid that James's first wife had been more interested in the Harris family fortune than her husband.

"Thank you for letting us use the freezer, by the way. I appreciated that."

The children's choir gave way to a handbell group, the ringing chimes filling the air as Rose waved off James's thanks, unwilling to accept praise for something so small.

"Your granddaddy was one of the kindest men I've ever met." Henry Harris had been one of the few people in Royal who had seen right through her act when she'd rebuffed her friends during those awful years after she'd married Edward. She couldn't bear for any of her former friends to know how Edward treated her, so she'd been cruel in the way she'd alienated everyone. But James's grandfather, a shrewd military veteran, had never bought the act. He'd kept right on being good to Rose. "You know if you ever need anything, you only have to ask. And what did you say the nanny's name was?"

She'd thought it sounded familiar.

"Lydia Walker." He lifted a hand in greeting to someone behind her as he said it. "Here she is now, in fact. She's helping me finish my holiday shopping today."

Rose turned, curious to see the woman who made James smile that way. There was a blatant male interest there that was hard to miss. And wasn't it interesting that James was out with the nanny—but no child in sight?

"Hello." The younger woman greeted her, extending her hand as she tucked a small shopping bag under her arm. Tall and slim, she wore a long skirt with boots and shawl-collar sweater, fashionable but down-to-earth. "I'm Lydia Walker, Mrs. Clayton. I recognize you from volunteering with the Family Fun Run you organized for the children's club last summer."

"Walker." Rose repeated it without meaning to, a trick that sometimes worked to jog a memory. She snapped her fingers as it came to her. "Wasn't that the name of the big bidder at the bachelor auction?" She had been stunned—along with the rest of the crowd—at the bid from the young woman. "What a tremendously generous donation to the charity."

Uh-oh. Apparently she'd stepped in it, based on the wary looks the two of them exchanged. As the awkward silence hovered, the scent of roasted chestnuts intensified with a vendor walking past with a silver concession cart. Fragrant smoke billowed to either side.

"Gail Walker is my sister," Lydia confirmed as she dodged a pair of little girls playing tag. "She definitely surprised us all with her bid."

Lydia's smile looked strained while James added, "But thanks to your grandson, Rose, the press coverage after the event really helped bring in more donations. The Pancreatic Cancer Research Foundation couldn't have asked for a better spokesperson than Daniel."

Rose was glad to hear it. But had the added donations been worth alienating her own grandson?

"Daniel isn't thrilled about being the 'Most Eligible Bachelor in Texas,' but he's been a good sport."

Rose traded a few more words with the two of them before they left to finish their holiday shopping. Her gaze followed James and Lydia, curious about the relationship that struck her as more than just professional. It was in the way they looked at one another. The way they stood close without touching.

The way they'd gone on a shopping outing without Teddy.

Not that it was any of her business. But Rose had learned a thing or two about the ways romance could grow between unsuspecting people over the years. Maybe she had an eye for matchmaking. She'd gained a keen eye for romance since it had been decidedly absent in her own life for so long.

But now, she had Gus.

Which reminded her, she needed to finish up her shopping, too.

She was about to enter Priceless, the antiques store in the big red barn that anchored the Courtyard Shops, when her phone vibrated. She pulled it from her jacket pocket to see a text from her grandson.

I'm getting more messages and deliveries every day from nutcases who want to meet me because of that damned article. From now on, I'm forwarding everything to the main house for you since this is what you wanted. I'm done.

Knowing how frustrated Daniel was sure didn't lift Rose's spirits. She'd only meant well by having the reporter write an article about Daniel. But he seemed more miserable than ever since she and Gus had orchestrated the breakup between him and Gus's granddaughter, Alexis Slade. At the time, they'd been so sure their feud would last forever, and their grandkids didn't belong together.

But she'd gone and fallen for Gus again in spite of herself. So what right did she have to keep Daniel and Alexis apart?

Maybe she didn't have such a good eye for matchmaking after all. One way or another, she and Gus needed to make this right for their grandchildren.

Listening to James on the phone with Teddy's babysitter, Lydia walked with him to his car parked near the Courtyard Shops.

"Just make sure you have the nursery monitor with you when you go downstairs," he explained to the young woman, his ranch foreman's daughter, who was home from college for the holidays. "I'm sure Mrs. Davis left some snacks for you on the counter."

Lydia smiled to hear him, thinking he was getting the hang of caring for his nephew. Ever since she'd started at the Harris house, she could see more ease in his interactions with the boy. But would his increased comfort level with his role prompt him to raise Teddy as his own?

Clearly, that had been his brother's preference.

Weaving between parked cars, she allowed her eyes to linger on James as they neared his vehicle. Memories of their kiss still made her breathless, sparking a fresh longing in her as she admired his athletic grace and powerfully built body. She'd agreed to the shopping outing when he had urged her to take some downtime away from the ranch, and she'd thought that was a good idea. Since she had some of her own Christmas shopping to do, she'd thought it could be fun to help him purchase gifts for Teddy while they had a sitter for the boy.

And it had been.

But she hadn't been prepared to field questions about Gail's bid from Rose Clayton. Not that Rose had questioned her, per se. Lydia had simply felt uncomfortable accepting any kind of "thanks" on Gail's behalf since her sister hadn't made the donation in the first place.

James had.

He finished up his call with the babysitter a moment later and pocketed his phone.

"The sitter is set for a few hours and I've got the feed from the nursery monitor on my phone." He opened the passenger door of the black BMW sedan. He'd already loaded the shopping bags in the backseat while she'd been preoccupied. "I had hoped I could talk you into dinner."

She hadn't expected the shopping outing to lead to more. And dinner definitely sounded like *more*. But after that kiss in his home theater, she'd been thinking about him all the time.

Imagining what might have happened if she hadn't retreated to her room that night.

"Dinner?" She met his gaze.

"The timing is perfect," he told her reasonably. Before he leaned fractionally closer, his voice lowering. "And I have been forthright about wanting to know you better."

A clear invitation.

Her heart beat faster.

"You have." She appreciated that. It made things easier with their working relationship that he'd put the ball in her court about how things would advance. Or not. "Can we just commit to that much? A get-to-know-you dinner?"

"Dinner only." He nodded as she slid into the passenger seat. "Dessert optional. I'm game. I'd like to spend a couple of hours learning more about what makes Lydia Walker tick."

His words circled around her mind as he walked to the driver's side door and started the car.

"You're serious about that?" She thought of all the men her mother had dated—and there had been many. She wondered if any of them had ever taken the time to really understand the real Fiona Walker.

She couldn't help but admire James for going to the effort.

"Of course. We should play a round of twenty questions or something. Make it fun."

The idea appealed to her, especially since she knew that James had been dealing with a lot recently. Not just the death of his sibling, but adjusting to a child in his life and the demands on his time from his relatively new position as Texas Cattleman's Club president.

Her own frustrations—mainly with Gail, but also with her mom—seemed small by comparison. Gail would come back to Royal sooner or later and Lydia would help her find a way to repay James if only in child care help. As for their mom, Lydia had to make Fiona understand she wasn't going to be a part of her wedding.

"I like it. Who goes first?" She didn't ask where they were going to dinner, although she was a little curious. It had been a long time since she'd been on a date.

And there was no denying it now that the shopping outing had turned to dinner—this *was* a date.

"Lydia, you wound me. Ladies first, of course."

"Sorry." She grinned as she shifted in her seat to see him better. "My usual male companions are in the one- to ten-year-old demographic, and they don't always have the manners you do. But if I'm going first, I want to know what you do for fun."

"For fun?"

"Yes. I've seen you work on the ranch and at the club. But even a busy man like you needs to unwind. And I know you don't take in a movie in the home theater since you've only used that for work."

He took his time thinking. "I used to do saddle bronc riding," he said finally. "I quit once I took on full responsibilities as the head of Double H, but I always enjoyed it."

There was a wistfulness in his voice that made her wonder how long it had been since responsibilities had consumed all his time. She wanted to learn so much more about him.

"You deserve a new hobby," she settled for saying instead.

"Inspire me, then. What do you do for fun?" He turned her question back on her as they drove under streetlights draped with wreaths and holiday lights.

"I'm a nanny. I play all the time."

"If you needed to unwind, I guarantee you peekaboo isn't your first choice for entertainment."

She smiled. "Point taken. I like hiking. I don't get to go often anymore, but growing up I liked taking my siblings onto the trails in the Ozarks."

"Sounds nice. Although you have to admit, you

might need to update your hobbies, too, if your best memories of hiking are from when you were growing up." He turned off the main road and it took her a moment to see the sign for The Bellamy.

"We can't have dinner here." She'd never been to the five-star resort inspired by George Vanderbilt's iconic French Renaissance chateau in North Carolina, but she'd seen photos and knew the place epitomized luxury.

"Of course we can. You like to visit the farmers market on Saturdays at the Courtyard Shops, right?"

She'd told him as much during their shopping outing today.

"Yes. And the farmers market is more my speed for a meal." Even at night, she could see the gorgeous, castle-like building looming ahead and all lit up. The stone turrets had huge holiday wreaths adorned with red bows, while white lights illuminated a massive poinsettia tree out front. So romantic. Anticipation heated through her.

"The Bellamy has a great farm-to-table restaurant, the Glass House. You'll love it." He was already pulling up to the valet stand.

"I'm not sure I'm dressed appropriately," she told him before he could lower the window.

"It's not overly glitzy, I promise." With the car in Park, he took her hand in his, his clasp firm and gentle all at once. "The emphasis is on great food, not decor. And you look beautiful."

She warmed at his words. She'd never been the glamorous type, but she appreciated that he saw beyond the superficial, that he saw *her*.

And wanted her.

"In that case, thank you," she said, her heart beating faster. "And based on our first round of questions, it seems like we owe it to ourselves to have some fun, don't we?"

"I'm on a mission tonight." He lifted her hand in his, kissing the back of it. "We're going to unwind and have fun."

Her skin tingled where his lips had touched her, leaving her breathless. For a moment, she forgot all about dinner, her brain stuck on the feel of his mouth on her. She'd signed on for this. Dinner. Getting to know him. A date.

And if a little shiver of nerves scuttled through her to think about what that meant—getting into a relationship with her boss—she chose to ignore it. She had worked hard. Like James, she'd taken on a lot of responsibilities at a young age. She'd always been the one to deny herself what she wanted to help out her family, while her mother and her sister certainly never thought twice about indulging themselves. Why couldn't she have a chance to do something a little wild? A little reckless?

If tonight presented her with a chance to simply

enjoy herself on the arm of a handsome man intent on charming her, Lydia wasn't going to refuse.

In fact, given how much she wanted him, she might be the one to suggest they go for dessert after all.

Eight

"This is amazing." Lydia closed her eyes after a bite of the wood-roasted mushrooms midway through their dinner, clearly savoring the experience.

James hadn't eaten at the Glass House before, but he had to admit he was impressed, too. The farm-to-table restaurant had a tasting menu and he'd talked her into trying it with him so they could see what they liked best. So far, there hadn't been a bad dish in the lot, each new plate boasting locally farmed fruits and vegetables, plus cheeses made on-site and wines from an extensive cellar. Lydia professed a special love of the mushroom dish, though, even after their waiter had delivered tasting plates of smoked trout, grilled guinea hen and roasted duck.

They sat at a quiet table in the back that overlooked The Bellamy grounds, including an ornamental garden decorated with white lights for the holidays. Inside, a pianist played in the front of the restaurant, the sound pleasantly dulled for conversing thanks to the live plants and potted trees that served as the main decor. Even inside, the Glass House was full of greenery.

"It's good to see you enjoying yourself since we now know that we both work too hard." He'd been surprised to realize how long it had been since he'd taken any time for fun when she'd asked him about it earlier.

Lydia sipped her wine, a pinot noir the sommelier had paired for this course.

"I'm very fulfilled by my work," she said as she replaced her glass on the table near a tray full of white votive candles and interspersed with white poinsettia blooms. "So I'm not sure that I necessarily devote too much time to it. But I could probably balance the job with more fun outlets."

"And yet your job with the child care facility will be different from what you've been doing, right?" he asked, liking the way she'd let her guard down tonight. "Why the change?"

"I thought it would be rewarding to oversee more children. To potentially touch more kids' lives than I could as a nanny." She pushed back from the table slightly, crossing her legs in a way that had her calf brush against his for a moment.

Her gaze darted to his, awareness from that touch pinging back and forth between them. Heat rising from even that brief contact. Was she finding it as tough to refrain from more as him? That kiss they'd shared was never far from his mind.

"Yet you've been taking care of kids your whole life. Or so it seemed to me when I read your mother's blog."

That flash of heat he'd seen in her eyes faded a bit, and he partially regretted bringing it up. But hadn't they said they were going to get to know each other?

"The *House Rules* empire is built on a whitewashed version of my family. The truth bears little resemblance to the fiction she posts online." She stopped speaking when their waiter neared to clear the plates from the meal and bring them the next round of the tasting menu, a selection of desserts.

The restaurant had grown more crowded since they'd started their meal, the muffled conversations of other diners rising though their corner of the room remained private.

Once the waiter left, Lydia dipped her spoon in the ginger ice cream while James wondered how to get their conversation back on track. He wanted Lydia first and foremost. But until she was ready for things to move forward between them, he would at least make sure he understood her more. Find out what made her tick.

"So you weren't involved with raising your siblings?" he asked, wondering how she could have faked all that knowledge she'd seemed to have in the videos online where she gave mini-lessons to parents on making homemade baby food or how to swaddle an infant.

"I was very involved," she clarified while he scooped some of the strawberry sorbet onto his plate. "But we weren't the carefree family my mother tried to pretend when she wrote blogs about our outings to the mountains or a day at the lake. While she was making daisy chain crowns with one kid for a good photo op, I was chasing six others to keep them from drowning or falling off a cliff."

He waited a beat to see if there was a follow-up to that story. An indication that she'd been exaggerating. But she simply swirled her spoon through the ice cream and took another bite.

"Didn't anyone else from your mother's business notice? Or get involved to help?"

"For years, there was no one else in the business. It wasn't until my late teens that the YouTube videos took off and started driving traffic to her blog, expanding her reach to what it is today." She set aside her spoon and leaned back in her seat while the pianist switched to a holiday tune on the far side of the restaurant.

Lydia's hazel eyes met his, and she swept a lock of her light brown hair away from her face. She wore a long skirt and a creamy-colored sweater belted at her waist, the shawl collar parting enough to show a hint of the pink tank she wore beneath it. A long gold necklace full of tiny charms nestled at the V of the sweater's opening, her initial glinting in tiny amber-colored stones on one of the pendants that dangled between her breasts.

"In that case, your mother owes a great deal to you for her success." He nudged a plate of green apple cobbler toward her to tempt her. "Not just for watching your siblings while she worked, but also for creating all those videos."

She arched an eyebrow at him. "Please don't tell me you watched any of my videos. I sound like the world's most pompous seventeen-year-old."

"I'm not going to lie. I was too curious about how to swaddle a baby to pass that one up. But I thought you sounded like a very knowledgeable young lady."

Shaking her head, she gave a wry laugh. "I made those videos after I argued with my mother. I told her she was doing her visitors a disservice by emphasizing child-centered learning to the point where her kids were no longer being parented. I thought she should provide more practical advice."

"So she let you do the work for her, and you made the videos." From what he'd seen when he visited the blog, Lydia's videos were the biggest draw.

"It was her way of putting my experience in my own hands," she said drily. "She would say that she gave me all the resources I needed to have a meaningful childhood. And she did give me a percentage of the advertising dollars that those videos made. But I always resented not being able to attend college full-time because I was scared to leave the younger kids unattended."

How different their childhood years had been. Lydia had been raised by a woman whom many people looked up to as a role model for motherhood, surrounded by siblings. James and his brother had been raised by nannies once their mother died, their father too involved with the ranch to spend time with his kids.

"And yet you went into a profession centered on children. You must look forward to having a family of your own one day."

The observation was automatic, and maybe too personal. But he was curious.

"One day," she acknowledged, a hint of wariness in her expression.

He wanted to know more about her, to ask more about her family, but she leaned closer to him then, her fingers sliding onto his wrist where his hand rested on the table. The contact robbed him of whatever he'd been about to say while her light fragrance teased him, stirring a different hunger.

"You're getting way ahead of me on the questions," she announced, her hair sliding forward as she tipped her forehead closer to his. "It must be my turn by now."

He wanted to kiss her. Would have kissed her if they were alone. Maybe it was just as well they'd spent the day together out in public. Because without Teddy around, he couldn't help but see Lydia as a desirable woman and not as his nephew's nanny.

"By all means." His voice lowered since she was so close to him. "Ask me anything."

She stared back at him, her hazel eyes reflecting the candlelight's glow. He lifted his free hand to smooth her silky hair away from her face so he could see her better. Or maybe he simply needed to touch her in some way.

When he tucked the strands behind her ear, he skimmed his fingertips down the side of her neck. Felt the wild race of her pulse just beneath her ear. Once they were alone, he promised himself he would kiss her right there, for a long, lingering taste.

Her eyelids fluttered even now, as if she could feel the burning imprint of his lips on her skin.

"I hope you mean that." She eased back a bit, nibbling on her lower lip as her hand slid away from his wrist. "Because I've been wondering where things stand with Teddy's grandparents. You said you'd reached out to them. Have they expressed an interest in taking him in?"

The question was a far cry from what he'd expected. But he'd been honest about wanting to know more about her. So he needed to let her understand him better, too. He'd made a mistake with his wife not to give her a clearer idea of what life would be like on the Double H. It would have benefited them both to discuss their expectations.

"I get the impression they're still grieving deeply for their daughter." He hadn't wanted to push them, but their lack of response the first time had made him send a follow-up letter. "They were still struggling with the loss, even though from what Parker told me, they were unhappy with her for marrying him in the first place and hadn't spoken to their daughter after the wedding."

Lydia shook her head, her expression showing dismay while the waiter cleared plates and refreshed their water.

"James, isn't that all the more reason for you to raise Teddy instead of them? You can't let that sweet baby go to a cold and unforgiving household who will have nothing positive to say about Teddy's father."

He didn't miss the hint of accusation in her voice. In her eyes.

"Parker always thought they'd come around."

James had trusted his brother's judgment of his in-laws. "They didn't necessarily dislike Parker, but they had planned for their daughter to marry the rancher with land neighboring theirs. Her marriage to my brother caused them to lose some of their acreage to the neighbor."

James hadn't remembered all the details since he'd been knee-deep in expanding the Double H at the time and marrying Raelynn. His focus had been on his own bride.

"That hardly seems like grounds for not speaking to your own daughter." Lydia toyed with the petal of one of the white poinsettias on the table, her pink manicured fingernail tracing the outline. "What if they cut Teddy off that way? Decide to stop speaking to him?"

James reached over to squeeze her hand, needing to reassure her. "I promise I would never let my nephew go into a home unless I was certain he would be raised with love."

He owed Parker that, and more.

Her eyes searched his. And whatever she saw there must have eased her concerns somewhat because some of the tension slid from her shoulders.

"Thank you." She nodded. Accepting. "Can I ask one more thing? Since you were ahead of me in the question game?"

"Is this one going to be as dicey as the last one?" He signed the tab the waiter had left on the table, and then sat back, wanting Lydia to feel comfortable talking to him.

He wasn't going to reach the level of intimacy he craved with her if she couldn't speak freely to him. And he wanted her more with each passing minute.

"Possibly." She recrossed her legs, her calf nudging his for a second time. "Can I still ask?"

Awareness flared from the contact. Hotter this time. His thoughts about what he wanted from this night threatened to derail his focus.

"Of course." He couldn't stop himself from threading his fingers through hers.

She stared at him in the candlelight, the loveliest woman he could imagine. Not just because of her looks, but because of her giving nature. Her warm heart. He wanted to lose himself in all that beautiful inner radiance.

But before she could ask him her next question, a feminine voice trilled from behind them.

"James Harris, you gorgeous man! Where've you been hiding?"

He recognized the voice of Cady Lawson, an outrageous flirt and an old friend. He knew exactly when Lydia spotted her because her luscious lips turned into a quick frown before an unreadable mask settled over her expression. She tugged her hand from his. Folded her arms across her chest.

Standing to introduce the women, James wondered how fast he could send Cady on her way so he could get this night back on track.

If Lydia had been the jealous type, she guessed the arrival of James's lady friend could have ruffled her feathers. Dressed in sleek white leather pants and a designer white silk blouse, the woman was beautiful enough to have walked out of the pages of a magazine. Glossy dark curls spilled over her shoulders, her natural beauty not needing any adornment as she flung her arms around James.

But as Lydia listened to James's introduction to Cady Lawson, a friend from his college days, Lydia could think only how grateful she was for the woman's timing. Lydia had been about to quiz James about the fact that he'd married a woman who hadn't wanted children—a significant detail she'd caught in that first conversation she'd had with him about his ex. But with all the heated awareness between them, and his tempting touches, she'd found herself wanting to back off a question that was probably—at this stage of their relationship—none of her business.

She'd used the twenty questions game to find out enough to know she cared about him, and that she appreciated his willingness to be forthright with her. Was it really necessary to have her every curiosity about him answered before she indulged in the attraction? No doubt her mother's haste to rush into relationships had made Lydia overly cautious.

At least, she hoped it had. She never wanted to be the kind of woman who catapulted into romance.

So even though James wore a wary expression as he conducted his conversation with the absurdly beautiful—and overtly flirtatious—Cady, Lydia found herself thankful for the reprieve from a dicey conversation. Apparently Cady was from Royal but lived in Dallas now, and had met a few friends at the Glass House for dinner.

"Well, I hope you know I would have attended that bachelor auction fundraiser if you'd been on the slate," Cady teased James, winking at Lydia. "I heard it through the grapevine that's why you took the Texas Cattleman's Club job as president. To keep yourself off the auction block."

Lydia found herself smiling. That sounded like the man who preferred to work over having fun.

They spoke for another moment before one of Cady's friends waved her back to their table.

"I really should go." She made a point of squeezing Lydia's shoulder in a friendly gesture. "It was nice meeting you, Lydia. Take care of him. He's a keeper."

The woman wouldn't have heard even if Lydia had tried to reply since she hurried away on metallic silver pumps that looked worthy of Cinderella herself. Instead, she glanced up at James, who could only shake his head.

"I'm sorry about that—"

Lydia cut him off and rose to her feet. "No need to apologize for having glamorous friends. I'm ready to go home, if you are."

"Of course. I hope you didn't feel rushed."

"Not at all." She slid her arm through the crook of his elbow, grateful for the chance to redirect the evening. "I was ready to leave."

"What about your question?" He readjusted her hand on his arm, covering it with his. Tucking her closer. "You were just about to throw me back in the hot seat."

She caught a hint of his aftershave as she glanced up at him, eye level with his jaw.

"I changed my question," she confided as he opened the door for her and passed the valet his ticket.

The cool night air made her step even closer to him and he wrapped his arm around her waist, his hand an inviting warmth on her hip.

"You did?" The question was a deep vibration of sound against her ear as he kissed her hair there.

Pleasurable shivers raced up and down her spine, his voice enticing her. She half wished the valet wouldn't return with the vehicle so they could stand this way longer.

Then again, the sooner the car came, the sooner

they'd be back at his home with the night ahead of them.

"Yes." She knew what she wanted, and she didn't want to be cautious about it anymore. "I just want to ask you, how fast can you get us home so we can be alone?"

As it happened, James had gotten them home very quickly.

Lydia hadn't realized that The Bellamy was so close to the Double H since they'd made a stop at the shops before dinner. A fire flamed hot inside her on the ride home, her body tense from holding back now that she'd decided to move forward with this out-of-control attraction. But before she knew it, James was steering the luxury sedan into the third bay of the ranch's main garage. The overhead door closed silently behind them.

"I just need to pay the sitter." He switched off the engine and exited the car, opening her door a moment later to offer his hand. "I'll meet you upstairs?"

She touched him only briefly, just enough to let him help her from the vehicle. If her hands lingered on him now, she feared she might not be able to pry herself away again.

As it was, his eyes dipped to her legs where her coat parted, the gaze smoking over her skin like a caress.

"Okay." She nodded, breathless from the contact. From thoughts of where tonight was going to lead. "I'll check on Teddy."

She hurried ahead of him when he let her inside the house, rushing up the stairs before she ran into one of the household staff or the sitter. She had used up all her restraint where this man was concerned, and she didn't want to risk any more delays.

Stopping by her room to shed her coat and her shoes, Lydia wondered if this was how her mother felt when she fell for a new man. Padding barefoot into her bathroom to run a brush through her windblown hair, Lydia recalled that it seemed like Fiona was in a mental fog when she met someone new. Her mom's starry-eyed attempts to get any work done were hampered by an inability to focus, an almost giddy preoccupation with the new man. Lydia had thought it looked more like a sickness than romance. But for the first time, as she stared into the mirror and her own bright eyes, she had an inkling of that sweetly off-balance feeling, a sensation no other man had ever stirred.

She hoped it was just because she'd ignored the attraction for so long. Surely that's why it felt so over the top.

Setting the hairbrush on the sleek white quartz counter beneath the rustic wood-framed mirror, Lydia left the bathroom to check on Teddy for the night.

The nursery door was slightly open, making it easy to slip into the boy's room. The new airplane night-light she'd bought for him glowed blue on the far side of the room, giving her enough light to see his face. Eyes closed, his arms rested on either side of his head, his green cotton sleeper snapped up to his neck. Lydia leaned over the crib to tug a lightweight blanket over his legs.

Turning on her heel, she almost ran into a solid wall of muscle and man.

James.

He steadied her shoulders, his hands an inviting warmth as they slid down her arms. She realized he'd taken off his shoes, too. No wonder she hadn't heard him on the plush carpet behind her.

"Sorry." He breathed the word into her ear before he glanced into the crib to see Teddy for himself. "Looks like he's down for the count."

Her heart beat too fast. James still held her hand, his fingers interlacing with hers.

"Is the sitter gone?" she asked, breathless and hoping that it sounded like she whispered on purpose.

"She is." He drew her out the door and into the hall with him before tugging her toward the master bedroom.

She hadn't seen that room on her tour of the house.

The arched double doors at the end of the corridor had been a source of intrigue for her other times during the past weeks. Now, as he turned the handle and opened them, she stepped over the threshold into his private retreat for the first time.

He let go of her hand to twist the lock, sealing them in the sitting area of the suite. Heavy linen curtains were drawn across one wall that she knew must be the bank of windows overlooking the front grounds. A stone fireplace held a stack of wood logs, and a steel-gray sectional sofa filled a corner near built-in bookshelves full of dark leather volumes. Framed paintings of stylized rodeo horses hung in a cluster above the mantel.

And, on the far side of the room, a massive four-poster bed.

James reached in the pocket of his jacket and withdrew the nursery monitor receiver. He set it on the wooden chest that served as a coffee table before returning to stand before her.

He made a point of checking his watch before he spoke.

"So, to answer your question from back at the restaurant, it seems I could have you home—and alone—in nineteen minutes." He relaxed his arms at his sides. Stepped fractionally closer. "I have to admit I'm curious where you wanted things to go from here."

Her heart beat so loudly now she could feel the

rush of blood in her ears, a vibration that drowned out everything else.

"Would you like me to be explicit?" She didn't know where she found that surge of boldness, but she smoothed the lapel of his jacket between her thumb and fingers, gliding up the fabric. "Or shall I just show you?"

She saw the flare of his nostrils. The way his pupils dilated so his eyes were almost black. She liked knowing she had that effect on him, too.

"I think I've gone past the point where I can handle anything explicit." He traced the line of her jaw with his knuckle, a teasing caress when she needed so much more. "I'll take the hands-on demonstration."

Heat tickled its way up her spine. And back down. Desire tantalizing her as her breathing grew ragged.

Arching up on her toes, she twined her arms around his neck, pressed herself to him and kissed him the way she'd been dying to for weeks.

Nine

Her kiss felt like he'd reached the oasis after a long slog through the dessert.

James let the sensations roll over him as he anchored her against him. Her vanilla-and-floral fragrance, the silky sweep of her hair feathering along his shoulders, the soft, feminine curves molding to the hard planes of his body. All of it was so damned scintillating.

And that kiss.

Her lips moved with a ravenous hunger he'd only guessed at in the weeks leading up to this moment. For so long, she'd been the consummate professional. So careful to present her capable, efficient side to the world, that seeing this facet of her reminded him that she'd trusted him with something special.

He refused to waste a second of it. Easing back to look at her, he placed a kiss on her cheek. Each of her closed eyes.

"Come with me." Releasing his hold on her, he took her hand and led her toward the bed.

She paused a second before following him, and he realized she was reaching for the nursery monitor. Would he have forgotten? Maybe. But surely they would have heard him even from the other side of the large suite.

She'd slipped off her boots earlier, and her feet were soundless on the floor behind him. Her long skirt swished against his calf, a teasing caress as they reached the edge of the mattress. He hit the remote by the bed to dim the lights except for the two sconces flanking the fireplace.

He waited while she set the nursery monitor beside the remote on the nightstand, reminding himself not to rush this. To savor every moment of having her here with him.

But Lydia wasn't waiting. Because her fingers were already unfastening the top button of his shirt, her lips pressing a kiss to the skin she bared. Propelling him to a new tier of craving for her.

Heat flared over his skin. He skimmed a touch down her shoulders, tugging at the belted sweater, parting the shawl collar until he could see more of the silky tank she wore beneath. He bent to kiss her neck, liking the way she arched into him. He felt her heartbeat race in the soft hollow below her ear. Lingered there until he nipped her earlobe and peeled her sweater the rest of the way down.

Her soft moan coincided with her fingers' speeding up on his shirt buttons. Her hips sidled against him, a sign of the same restless ache he was feeling. An ache that had become second nature to him in the last week. The trip to Houston hadn't helped him douse it. If anything, time apart had only made him want her more.

With a fierceness he'd never felt for any woman.

Maybe that's why he was so careful not to let that hunger rule him now. Being with Lydia felt like uncharted terrain for him. An all-new experience.

"More naked," she demanded against his ear, her voice a breathless whisper he couldn't ignore.

He tugged her sweater off. Skimmed the silky tank up over her head, leaving her in the long skirt and a band of sheer lace around her breasts. The rosy peaks of her nipples tempted him, but Lydia was already sliding his shirt off.

"I meant you," she clarified, twisting to unfasten a hook on the side of her skirt that sent the pleated wool to the floor almost at the same time as his shirt joined it. "It's you who needs to be more naked."

She moved quickly now that she'd made up her mind to go through with this night, but James had been waiting so long to touch her he wanted to savor everything about her.

Sheer gray lace hugged her hips at the juncture of long, slender legs. The sight of her made him realize that taking his time wasn't going to work. Not when she trembled that way, her fingers jittery with anticipation and need.

He reeled her closer, wrapping her in his arms. Kissing her until some of that tension turned hot. Molten. She gripped his shoulders and he lifted her up, clamping an arm around her waist. He reached behind them to rake back the covers before he laid her down, her hair spilling over the pillowcase.

Lying down beside her, he kissed and touched her, finding the places she liked best. A kiss under her ear. A touch on the curve of her hip. Skimming across her belly. Cupping the lace between her legs.

The soft, whimpering sounds she made while he caressed her fueled his restraint, every throaty sigh steeling his resolve to wait. To bring her pleasure first. Ignoring the heated ache for her, he shifted all his focus on Lydia.

Ever so slowly, he rolled away the thin lace barrier over her breasts so he could tease one nipple with his tongue. She wrapped a hand around his back, palm splayed, holding him close. Drawing on the taut peak harder, he slid aside the lace between her legs, stroking her there.

Her breathing grew harsh, her short nails grazing his skin. Her back arched, her hips pushing against his hand until the tension broke in lush spasms that racked her whole body. A beautiful release that filled him with as much satisfaction as any of his own. He kissed her neck in the aftermath, holding her close until her heartbeat slowed a little.

Still a little dazed by the sweet shimmer of every nerve ending, Lydia had almost caught her breath when he slid out of bed. Before she could protest, she watched as his hands moved to his belt.

Just like that, the heat inside her flared again. That fast, her body reminded her of a new ache. The hunger for him returning. Wriggling out of her twisted lace underthings, she shed her clothes while he tossed aside the rest of his and returned to the mattress beside her.

He placed a condom on the nightstand. Gauntlet dropped.

She wrapped herself around him, arms twining behind his neck while he rolled her on top. She could feel how ready he was for her and it sent another shiver through her. Anticipation mingling with breathless desire.

When he kissed her this time, there was no holding back. No careful wait while she found release. This kiss was hungrier, a little less controlled. And she loved it.

She explored his body with her hands and mouth, reveling in the perfectly formed muscle, the taut strength evident with every flex and movement. When she kissed lower, though, tempted to give him the same kind of pleasure he'd shown her, he rolled her to her back. Pinning her briefly to the bed before he knelt up to find the condom on the nightstand.

She arched against him, hurrying him with frenzied movements of her hips. Her hands. She couldn't wait another moment.

And then, finally, he made room for himself between her legs. Entered her with a slow, perfect slide of their bodies together. The sensation stole her breath, her body slowly accommodating him while ribbons of pleasure trickled through her. She closed her eyes, savoring it, wanting to hold on to it for as long as she could.

But he started moving, and the magic of that only took her higher. Hotter. She was mindless again, all caution shredded and burnt to ashes as she clung to him, chanting her pleasure against his ear while they drove each other wild.

By the time he took her hands in his, holding

them over her head while he kissed her, she was lost to everything but this moment and the man. He reared back to look at her, his dark eyes locking on her for a long moment before he lowered his head to suckle her breast.

Sending her catapulting over the edge, release sweeping through her in one exquisite wave after another.

She wasn't sure if the squeeze of her body was what spurred his release or if he'd been that close already, but their voices mingled in a hoarse song of fulfillment. His a throaty shout, hers a high cry of perfect bliss.

He rolled to her side afterward, tucking her against him while she breathed in the scent of his skin. His jaw rested on her hair, the slight bristle of whiskers catching on her hair. She nuzzled deeper into the crook of his neck, more content than she had a right to be.

But she refused to think about that now. Not when everything inside her glowed with pleasure. She planned to hold on to this feeling for as long as she could. To simply be.

As their breathing slowed and Lydia thought she might doze off, a wail erupted from the speaker on the baby monitor.

A real-world reminder that this night hadn't changed anything and that she still had a job to do.

Nothing could have brought home faster the fact that she'd just slept with her boss.

But even as she righted herself to find her clothes, James gently pressed her shoulders back to the mattress.

"I'll get him." He brushed a caress over her hair. Kissed her forehead. "Don't go anywhere."

She thought about protesting, since she really didn't mind. She had missed Teddy today while he'd been with the sitter and she found herself looking forward to seeing him, if only to comfort him for a few minutes before putting him back to bed. But her nanny training told her it would be better for James to do that. To build the bond between the toddler and the man Lydia hoped would become his father.

"Okay." She smiled as James stepped into his boxers and shrugged his way into a T-shirt. "Thank you."

But as she watched him scoop up his phone and leave the room, she couldn't help but think it strange that her professional life had dictated her actions now instead of her personal preferences. Even though this evening had been the furthest thing from professional.

Tucking the covers higher under her chin, Lydia hoped she could figure out a way to balance the two sides sooner rather than later. Because she'd just experienced only her first taste of behaving with a little reckless abandon. She couldn't bear to return to her careful, cautious self just yet.

James paced around the nursery with his nephew asleep on his shoulder half an hour later, not ready to put him back in his crib quite yet.

Part of the reason was because he guessed Lydia would have dozed off by now, too, so no need to rush. But the other reason that had him still pacing? He knew that bringing Lydia to his bed tonight would have repercussions. She wasn't a woman to get involved lightly. He knew that in his bones. Yet here he was, risking losing a nanny he desperately needed just to be with her.

He tipped his cheek to his nephew's curls, stroking the baby's back while he stared at the stuffed felt figures that Lydia had strung along one wall. A bunny in a Santa hat. A couple of cats dressed like elves, one hammering a toy train and the other sewing a doll. She was so good at her job. Compassionate. Warmhearted.

She had come into James's life for Teddy's sake, but she'd brought a whole lot of happiness for both of them. Was it fair to Teddy to deprive the boy of Lydia if he went to live with his maternal grandparents? Thinking about parting with the child was getting tougher every day, but James had to do what was best for him.

Settling the baby back into the crib, James stepped

out of the nursery and into the hall to check his phone. He'd seen a message from Teddy's grandmother while they'd been out shopping, but he hadn't responded to her yet. He reread it now.

We gratefully accept your invitation to spend the new year with our grandson, Samantha Mason had written in a short email. We will be arriving in midafternoon on New Year's Eve and can watch Teddy for you that evening and the next day. Thank you for opening your home to us so we can get to know our grandson.

There was nothing in the note about taking Teddy full-time. But James understood they wanted to meet the boy first. Still, it shouldn't be like a job interview where Teddy had to perform well in order for his grandparents to want to raise him.

Either they wanted the child or not.

Still, this was a step in the right direction, he hoped. Teddy needed a more stable family than what James could provide. Plus, he deserved the tender touch of a mother figure in his life.

Opening an email screen for a response to Mrs. Mason, James tapped out a quick reply, confirming the details of their trip to Royal. The annual Texas Cattleman's Club New Year's Eve Ball was that night, and this way, Lydia would be available to accompany him.

James clicked the button to send the email and then strode back to the bedroom. He knew Lydia wanted to attend the New Year's Eve Ball for networking purposes, to find potential clients for the day care business she would open next fall. But he hoped she would be pleased to attend as his guest so they could share more incredible nights like this one.

He looked forward to thinking about how to invite her. Maybe with an extravagant Christmas present as a hint—earrings or a necklace, something beautiful to wear—could be his segue to asking her.

They had a lot of fun ahead of them. Together.

But first things first, he planned to slide back into his bed beside her. Kiss her. Touch her. Wake her slowly, in the most seductive way imaginable.

Ten

Christmas Eve day passed in a whirl of holiday preparations, and Lydia had so much fun with James and Teddy that she felt a twinge of guilt by the time the evening rolled around. She hadn't phoned her mother. Hadn't tried calling Gail.

But as she watched Teddy and James lying side by side in the living room, making "snow" angels in giant piles of cotton balls, she couldn't muster much regret about her family. They hadn't phoned her either. A fact that made her wonder why she always had to be the one to give. Was it so wrong to soak up the fun with the Harris males? One, a giggling, overtired toddler patting the cotton ball snow onto his head. The other, an exceedingly attractive rancher who had hurdled all her defenses and inspired her to start thinking about her own wants for a change.

Maybe it was high time she did just that.

Seeing how much fun her two companions were having while they played at least reassured her she'd done one thing right in helping James to be more comfortable in his father role. There was no denying he was good at this.

"Mrs. Davis is going to wonder what happened when she gets home from her holiday with family and finds cotton everywhere for the next two weeks," James observed as he sat up. Fluffy white balls rolled off his shoulders, disappearing under the sofa.

For her part, Lydia was happy to have the house to themselves for three whole days. The cook, the housekeeper and the extra part-time staffers were all on vacation for Christmas. At least now she didn't have to pretend there was nothing going on between her and her sexy employer.

"I'll vacuum it up," she assured him, her gaze wandering over him appreciatively. "It was my idea."

"You're not allowed to clean." Something heated glinted in his eyes as he leaned closer to her, kissing her hands where they rested on her knees. "I'm pulling rank on you with that one. Besides, we can turn the cotton into a tree skirt, right?" He shoved a pile closer to the fifteen-foot Fraser fir near the windows. "It will look like it snowed in here."

"What should we do with the tired little boy in the middle of the floor?" She smiled to see Teddy carefully pulling apart a cotton ball, his fingers picking at the fluffy strands before he waved a hand impatiently to remove the tufts.

James was already on his feet, scooping Teddy up in his big, strong arms. "I'll only put him in bed if I can trust you not to clean anything while I'm gone."

Lydia rose, following him so she could wipe the remnants from the baby. "It's a deal, but let me make sure he doesn't have any extra pieces on him." She picked off a few bits clinging to his sleeper, making Teddy giggle. Then she carefully examined his hands. "My little sister got a strand of hair wrapped around her toe once inside her footie pajamas, and we had to take her to the ER to have the hair removed."

"You went to the ER for a strand of hair?"

"When it winds tightly enough, it can cut off circulation." She stepped back. "But he looks good to me."

James shook his head as he spoke to Teddy. "Champ, it looks like we're going to have to change your sleeper and examine all your toes now." He glanced back at Lydia before he started up the stairs. "And I've got an early present for *you* when I'm done. Don't go anywhere."

Something about the tone of his voice sent a shiver of awareness through her. Waking up in his arms this morning had felt incredibly decadent. Making love in the shower while Teddy napped had been even more self-indulgent. Still...

She could get used to it.

Not that she'd have the chance since this window of time with James was only temporary. Soon enough, the holidays would end, her sister would return and Lydia would convince Gail to step up and take over the nanny duties with Teddy. After all, it was still Gail who owed the debt to James, and Lydia had faith her sister would do what she could to pay him back for generously covering her donation. But could Lydia maintain a relationship with James if she was no longer working for him?

The idea tempted her.

Being with James had made her take more chances, and so far, she had reaped wonderful rewards from her gambles. Continuing to see him, to date, would be an even bigger risk. She'd never wanted to turn into a woman like her mother, falling head over heels at the drop of a hat. Yet what Lydia had with James seemed so much different from that. So much more special.

Sure, she may have felt like she'd rushed into an intimate relationship. But in comparison with how fast her mom normally moved from dating to the altar, Lydia had practically proceeded at a snail's pace.

She corralled a few rogue snowballs under the tree, liking the idea of a snowy tree skirt. Teddy had so much fun playing with the fake snow anyway, he would enjoy it tomorrow, too.

James's deep voice behind her sent a thrill through her. "Remember what I said about no cleaning?"

His arms went around her a moment later and she forgot everything but being with him. About falling for him. Maybe it would be simpler if it was just about the heated connection they shared. But that didn't begin to account for her growing feelings for this incredible man. The tenderness she experienced when she watched him play with his nephew. The respect she had for his generosity and his work ethic.

She couldn't pretend what she felt was simply attraction.

"I don't think you can boss me around when I'm not technically working now," she teased. Tipping her head back to his chest, she rubbed her cheek against all that hard strength. "And I think we'll have more fun tonight if I remain off-duty, don't you?"

"Yes." He spun her in his arms so she faced him. His eyes probed hers, his expression more serious than she'd expected. "I've been looking forward to tonight all day."

His hand cupped her cheek, cradling her face. Her heart stuttered a jerky rhythm. Had Gail felt anything close to this when she ran off on a weeks-long vacation with her bachelor?

If so, maybe Lydia owed her the tiniest bit of slack. Because right now, she could almost imagine turning her back on everything to be with him.

"Me, too," she told him honestly. As much fun as she'd had preparing for Christmas and playing with Teddy today, she'd be lying if she said she wasn't looking forward to a repeat of the night before.

The chance to be in James's arms.

"But first…" He let go of her to lead her toward the Christmas tree. "…presents."

He guided her toward the big leather sofa closest to the pine branches and waited while she took a seat. She tucked the skirt of her burgundy-colored sweater dress closer to her while she watched him retrieve a small box from the back of the tree.

Wrapped in gold foil painted with white snowflakes, the paper was elegant, the package itself curiously shaped. He handed it to her, and she could feel a flat square on one side, and a heavier square against it. Almost like he'd wrapped a card.

"I only have one gift for you," she protested, wondering if she should retrieve it. "Shouldn't I wait to open this until tomorrow?"

He lowered himself onto the sofa beside her, his hand sliding around her waist. "No. This is a bonus present for tonight. Something I wanted you to have sooner rather than later."

How quickly she'd grown used to his touch. She leaned into it now while she slid a finger into the wrapping, not wanting to tear it needlessly. Inside, there was a card with her name on it along with a smaller box. But why had he wrapped the card?

She glanced over at him, but his expression gave nothing away as he waited. Opening the envelope, she saw it wasn't a greeting card, but an invitation.

"The Texas Cattleman's Club New Year's Eve Ball?" She read the embossed letters aloud. It was one of the most anticipated and prestigious events in Royal. "Really?"

"I want you to be my date," he added. "It should be fun, and I think it would really help you meet potential clients for the child care facility."

"That's very generous of you." She was touched that he'd thought of the business that meant so much to her. "I would be honored to be there."

She didn't know what the date said about their new relationship, but he must realize that taking his nanny to the New Year's Eve Ball would be a very public way to acknowledge their relationship. Surely that implied the same level of seriousness she felt about him?

"Good." He kissed her temple and squeezed her

waist a little tighter, hugging her. "Then open the next part of the gift."

Excited, she opened the foil paper carefully, then lifted the lid on a yellow-and-red box. Inside, nestled on a velvet cushion, rested an old-fashioned hair comb in art deco style, with crystals outlining three tiny skyscraper buildings.

"James, it's beautiful," she breathed, already imagining how she could wear her hair to show off the piece.

"It belonged to my mother. I have a photo of her and my father on New Year's Eve with that comb in her hair, and I would like you to have it."

Overwhelmed from the magnitude of the gesture, she shook her head. "I couldn't possibly accept a family heirloom—"

"Please." He laid his hand on her forearm. "She had an extensive collection of jewelry, and I think your kindness to her grandson warrants a thank-you. I know she would be as grateful to you as I am for all you've done to help Teddy."

Blinking away the sudden moisture in her eyes, she smiled. "In that case, thank you. I will treasure it."

She felt something shift inside her. A tender place in her heart that was just for this man. Or maybe it was the last of her defenses crumbling in the face of his warmth and generosity. No one had ever put her first the way he did.

Maybe that's why it was so easy to lose herself

in his kiss when he captured her chin in one strong hand. Because giving in to the heated attraction, and the simplicity of that connection, was easier than trusting the feelings for him multiplying with every moment they spent together.

James didn't waste a second coaxing Lydia up the stairs when he wanted her right here. Right Now.

The front door was locked. He had the nursery monitor feed on his phone. So he dragged the cashmere blanket from the arm of a nearby chair and spread it out on the leather sofa behind her before he gently lowered her there.

They'd been together on multiple occasions since that first electric encounter. But far from quenching his hunger for her, each time only made him want her more.

Lydia's frenzied touches were as desperate as his own, as if not touching for hours all day long drove them to this frantic shedding of clothes. His shirt. Her shoes. He didn't even bother removing her sweater dress. Between her wriggling and his greedy hands, they had the fabric up around her waist in no time.

"Condom?" she rasped against his lips, not even bothering to open her eyes while they kissed.

"Mmm." He reached in his pocket to put the packet in her hand since he didn't feel like breaking that kiss either.

He'd waited all day to have her mouth on him.

She must have set the packet aside, because her hands wandered over his fly, stroking and seeking, speeding his pulse to a drumroll. He helped her only to save himself from the zipper, but he appreciated her desire that echoed his own. The way she touched him threatened his control.

Together, they made quick work of his pants. Her panties. And, for expediency's sake, he ended up with her straddling his lap while he rolled the condom into place.

Her hands laced behind his neck, thighs bracketing his hips as he slid inside her. She tipped her forehead to his, holding herself very still for a long moment. He waited, need for her burning through him. But when she started to move, the sweetness of it made him want to give her free rein with him. She kissed her way up his neck. His jaw. All the while moving with a hypnotic grace that had him seeing stars.

It was too soon.

He'd hardly even touched her yet. But she seemed intent on her course, pinning his hands to the sofa cushion with the light press of her fingers. Her breath was a sweet brush of air along his earlobe when she told him how good it felt.

He closed his eyes, scavenging for the control he'd exercised the night before. But between her soft words, the gentle glide of her hips and the way her fingers circled his wrists, he was burning from the inside out. He kissed her deeply, then trailed his lips down her neck to her breast. He captured the peak with his mouth, feeling the answering shiver that coursed through her right before her release hit her.

He focused on the feel of it, her body throbbing all around him, drawing him deeper. Squeezing. He couldn't have held out another second, his own completion surging hard.

He banded his arms around her, anchoring her to him while the passion burned white hot. Leaving him spent and sagging into her. Strands of her hair clung to his skin as she laid her head on his shoulder. He kissed the top of her head, wanting to carry her to his bed. To wrap her in his arms and his blankets.

"That was just a warm-up," he assured her, drawing the cashmere throw up to her shoulders.

She gave a soft laugh as she disentangled herself from him and dressed. "In that case, I'm not sure I'd survive the main event. Besides, we have Christmas presents to bring downstairs. I know Teddy is young, but he will be excited to see all the packages in the morning."

James admired her commitment to making the day special for the boy. "You're a pretty great nanny." He slid on his boxers and pants. "The women who looked after Parker and me never gave much thought to our holidays."

She regarded him silently, as if waiting for

more. Making him realize how self-pitying that had sounded.

Damn.

"We had great holidays thanks to my dad." It was sort of true. Christmas was one of the few days their father didn't work. "I only pointed it out to let you know you're very generous with your time and attention."

"Every child deserves happy holiday memories." She folded her arms around herself. "And Teddy is all the more special to me because he's your family."

Her words chased around his head long after they went upstairs to bring down the presents they'd wrapped from their shopping outing, distracting him. He tried picking them apart, to figure out what it was about her statement that troubled him.

It was good she cared about his nephew.

And yes, James was grateful that she cared about him, too.

But if she was already this attached to the boy, would Lydia understand if James followed through on his resolution to let Teddy's grandparents raise him?

He had a week before the New Year's Eve Ball when the Masons arrived in town to watch Teddy for the night. He hoped it would be enough time for him to find a way to tell her that if things went well with the Masons, he wouldn't need a nanny anymore.

Eleven

Christmas Day got off to a fitful start.

Lydia hoped Teddy was just teething, but he remained grumpy and unimpressed by the holidays. He'd made grouchy sounds off and on while he played with a toy train, gripping it tightly in his hand as he pushed it around and around the floor.

She hoped it was just the toddler's irritability that made the day feel awkward. At noontime, over brunch fare in the large, eat-in kitchen, she traced an idle finger over the natural wood grain in the Texas ebony slab polished into a tabletop. Yet she returned her gaze to James again and again, wondering if something had shifted between them the day before.

James had participated fully in the cooking and preparations for the meal, but as she halfheartedly nibbled a bite of her French toast, she tried to pinpoint when things had begun to feel strained. His words about his own Christmases—that his nannies hadn't participated in the holidays—had made her wonder if she'd overstepped his expectations for her role here.

She'd always been very involved with her charges, imagining a child would thrive with that warmth of connection to a caregiver. She'd received a degree in early childhood development, patching together enough online coursework for her bachelor's over the years. But her real source of knowledge about child care came from her years in Arkansas, helping to raise her brothers and sisters. But had she brought too much of her own experience with her siblings into her nannying? Too much familiarity?

Then again, maybe James's own background skewed his perception of her role here. He'd lost his mother early and hadn't been close with his caregivers. He had loved and married a woman who hadn't wanted children, after all. A fact she'd never asked him about.

Maybe it was past time she did. Because she adored children and had crafted a profession around them. One day, she dreamed of a family of her own.

Shoving aside her half-eaten plate, she sipped

her sparkling water with orange and debated how to be tactful.

The doorbell's resonant chime interrupted her thoughts.

James frowned, setting down his fork. "I wasn't expecting anyone."

Teddy piped up from his high chair where he spun the wheels on his toy train. "Hel-lo?" he asked, his brown eyes turning to Lydia. "Hello?" He opened and closed his hand in a baby wave.

Her heart melted to see him make that connection, his eyes wide with curiosity as he watched James leave the room to answer the door. The small moment made her more certain of herself and the way she did her job. Forming a bond with children she cared for was only natural. Even if she didn't have strong feelings for James, his nephew would hold a piece of her heart.

"Do you want to say hello?" she asked him, getting to her feet. "We can go see who's here."

"Who. Here." He banged his train on the tray of the high chair. "Here. Here. Here."

Lydia unbuckled Teddy's safety belt and lifted him. He hadn't eaten anything besides a few pieces of dry cereal, so he was clean enough. She settled him on her hip, straightening his navy blue reindeer sweater before striding toward the living area.

"Merry Christmas!" a feminine voice trilled

from the front room as James opened the door for their guest.

Lydia's sister Gail breezed right into the house, dressed in a poinsettia-printed skirt and fuzzy red sweater. Tanned and sporting fresh caramel-colored highlights in her dark brown hair, Gail wore leather boots that appeared brand-new. Worst of all? The woman who owed a hundred thousand dollars to James came with her arms full of lavishly wrapped Christmas presents.

James appeared too surprised to return her greeting. Then again, maybe he didn't even remember what she looked like since the bachelor auction had been a month ago.

"James." Lydia cleared her throat and hurried closer, mortified that her sister would think it was okay to come by unannounced on Christmas, waltzing into James's house like a conquering hero, when she'd ignored his calls and the messages from the Pancreatic Cancer Research Foundation. "You remember my sister Gail?"

"Of course." Stepping forward, he recovered himself quickly. "Let me help you with those."

"Thank you!" Gail gushed, handing over the stack of boxes and a shopping bag to James. "I don't think we had the chance to speak at the charity event. You were a wonderful MC for the auction."

Gail's hazel eyes were bright and clear, her gaze direct as she strode deeper into the living area. As if she had absolutely no conscience about what she'd done. In that moment, with her sunny smile and perfectly primped brown curls, she bore a striking resemblance to their mother. Even her voice, relentlessly upbeat as if she could deliver a House Rules podcast at any moment, reminded Lydia of Fiona Walker.

Or maybe it was simply that, no matter how much Lydia had tried to teach her siblings about hard work and practical values, Gail preferred the laissez-faire approach to life. Both Fiona and Gail were determined that things would "work themselves out." Even astronomical bids for bachelors with money you didn't have.

Incensed, Lydia couldn't seem to make her feet move from where she stood in Gail's way, blocking her from the living area where James was putting the packages under the Christmas tree.

"He wasn't just the MC, Gail." Lydia hadn't planned to confront her sister. But the realization that Gail had turned out exactly like their mother rattled Lydia to her core. Why did she keep trying to fix her family's messes when they let her down time and time again? "As the president of the Texas Cattleman's Club, James was also the main liaison for the charity when they hosted the bachelor auction."

"Is that right?" Gail stopped her forward momentum, her smile faltering only for a moment.

"How nice. Mom told me you were working here now, so I hoped we could spend some family time together. It *is* Christmas."

Teddy bounced in Lydia's arms, ready to be put down.

James moved closer, reaching for his nephew. "I can take him so you two can visit."

She handed over the child, anger at her sister building as she kept her focus on Gail. "Do you know *why* I'm working here now?"

James palmed her lower back, speaking to her quietly. "Lydia, there's no need to go into that just yet."

She disagreed. Because if Gail was audacious enough to stride in here and play the benevolent sister while Lydia worked to repay Gail's debt, a conversation was warranted.

Gail's expression shifted to something that looked like concern. "I've always known how much you enjoy children, Lydia. You have since we were little girls playing with baby dolls."

"Ba-by?" Teddy asked, bouncing excitedly in James's arms.

Lydia tensed, realizing her sister's view of their shared past was too far from her own to ever be reconciled.

"No, Gail." She dragged in a deep breath to cool down the fiery frustration. "I'm working here to help repay James, who covered your outrageous bid at the bachelor auction."

"Ba-by! Ba-by!" Teddy shouted, wriggling so hard that James had to let him down to run around the Christmas tree, his light-up sneakers flashing red and blue.

She guessed James was probably glad for the chance to escape the confrontation as he chased Teddy. Lydia hadn't meant to put him in the middle of this. Then again, she hadn't expected her sister to arrive on Christmas Day, pretending nothing had happened.

"Why would you do that?" Gail studied her, shaking her head. She spared a glance for James, who'd moved to the far side of the room where Teddy had tried to hide behind a chair.

"Why?" Exasperated, Lydia paced in a circle. "Because it's the right thing to do. Because I don't want our name attached to bad debts while we're trying to get new businesses off the ground. This is a small town. Word gets around."

"But I didn't ask for help. And I told you I'd figure things out after vacation." Gail squeezed her arm. "I can tell this is a bad time. I should have known you don't like spontaneous visits."

An old dig. Her mother had always thought that the reason Lydia didn't like impulsive family outings was because she couldn't be "spontaneous." When the truth was she simply preferred to have sunscreen packed so the kids didn't end up with third-degree burns from a day at the beach. Or she liked having swimming vests for the little ones since there were too many of them to keep an eye on in the water.

But Fiona—and apparently Gail—preferred to think Lydia was just no fun. Overly cautious. Turning on the heel of her new leather boots, Gail headed for the door. The movement shook Lydia from her thoughts.

"So you're leaving again? Without figuring out anything?" Lydia followed her sister toward the foyer, feeling as frustrated as Teddy had this morning. It was a good thing she wasn't carrying around a toy train or she would have been tempted to throw it the way the toddler had during the gift-opening.

What was it about family that could catapult a person right back to childhood dynamics?

"Why should I try to figure it out?" Gail asked over her shoulder, her hand on the big brass handle. "You'd only do a better job of it than I would anyhow." She lifted a hand to her mouth as she called back to the living area, "Merry Christmas, James!"

Lydia felt the steam hiss slowly from her ears. "Gail, we need to talk."

"You should ask James to take you to the New Year's Eve Ball at the Texas Cattleman's Club. Lloyd and I will be there." Gail grinned again, her happiness irrepressible in the face of everything. "I'm over the moon about him."

And then Gail was gone. Sauntering off to her compact car decorated with a wreath on the grill.

Something about the vehicle, her sister's joy, even her "spontaneity," made Lydia feel like Scrooge by comparison.

"Are you all right?" James's voice over her shoulder made her realize she'd been standing at the closed door for too long.

She hadn't even heard him approach.

Pivoting to face him while he held Teddy, Lydia felt her chest squeeze with a mixture of fierce attraction and soul-deep affection. She'd come to care for him so much. So fast.

I'm over the moon about him.

Gail's comment circled around Lydia's brain, the only words her sister had spoken today that Lydia could identify with. She knew the feeling all too well. Because she felt it for the generous, hardworking man standing in front of her.

She was over the moon for James Harris. And just as quickly as Gail had plunged into her own whirlwind relationship.

The idea of sharing something in common with her impulsive sister triggered a flicker of anxiety in her chest.

"I'm—not sure." She wanted to step into the warmth and comfort of his arms. But given that she'd known James for an even shorter length of time than Gail had known Lloyd Richardson, did that make Lydia's feeling imprudent? Unwise? "I mean, I'm upset. Obviously."

She'd never had a panic attack before, but she wondered if this was how it started. She felt unsettled. Nervous. Fidgety. She swallowed fast and tried to catch her breath.

"Why don't you come sit?" James juggled Teddy in his arms and gestured in the direction of the kitchen. "We can finish our brunch. Talk."

That sounded reasonable. Because James was a reasonable, rational person, like her. She clung to the idea with both hands as she followed him toward the kitchen. At least she hadn't bid money she didn't have to win a date with him.

No, she only started an affair with her employer. Which, for all of her mother's hasty relationships, even Fiona had never done.

"Do you think we jumped into things too quickly?" Lydia asked as James carefully settled Teddy in his high chair.

"I think *quickly* is subjective." He seemed to choose the words carefully.

"You're right." She appreciated his thoughtful response.

Some of the worry in her chest eased. James was a good man, and just because she'd developed strong feelings for him didn't mean she was turning into her mother.

She hoped.

"Can I warm up your plate?" he asked, his hand resting on her shoulder for a moment. "Or get you something else to eat?"

His touch settled her and stirred her at the same time. But she resisted the urge to tip her head against his forearm and soak in the comfort of his presence.

"No, thank you." She returned to her seat at the long table, hoping they could address some of the things that had troubled her earlier. "I'll just have some fruit."

She appreciated the distraction of Teddy banging his train on the high chair tray while she spooned a few pieces of fruit into a serving bowl.

"I thought I heard your sister mention the New Year's Eve Ball." James helped himself to more orange juice from a glass pitcher.

"She'll be attending with Lloyd," she confirmed, wishing they could rewind time. Somehow find more even footing again. "I hope that's not too awkward."

"Of course not." He sounded sincere. "Lydia, I made the donation because handling it that way was easiest for me. I'm not worried about anyone repaying the debt."

He'd told her that before. All along, he'd been willing to forgive the debt and simply pay her to be Teddy's nanny.

"That's very generous of you."

"It also served my best interests since I was drowning in my grief and obligations, feeling like I was failing on all fronts." He took her hand in his. Stroked his thumb along her knuckles. "I am so grateful to you for getting me through these last few weeks, Lydia. But it's still my hope that Teddy's maternal grandparents will welcome him into their home and be able to give him all the time and attention he needs."

The gentle caress of his thumb was at odds with the discordant crash of his words through her.

"You still plan to give him up?" She couldn't have possibly heard him correctly.

"The Masons are driving down from Amarillo to watch Teddy on New Year's Eve so we can attend the ball," he explained. "If things go well that night, we can start discussing how to make the transition—"

"You don't want him." She wrenched her hand from his as the harsh truth smashed through her romantic hopes and the tender feelings she'd developed for James. "You never wanted children in the first place."

"That's not true." He sat back in his chair, the space between them feeling five times bigger than the physical distance. "I will keep Teddy if things don't work out with the Masons."

"Even though your brother wanted you to raise him, you're still considering giving him up?" Hurt and anger propelled the question from her even though it was a low blow. That she wasn't being fair.

But how was he being fair to Teddy, who'd so clearly bonded with James? The child had already suffered a devastating loss with the death of his parents. How would he cope with more feelings of abandonment?

James held himself very still. Calm and controlled in the face of her anger. "You of all people should understand that our siblings don't always know what's best."

Begrudgingly, she nodded, acknowledging the point even if she didn't like it. "You're right. But I'd like to ask you one more thing. Just so I understand you better."

She had to put a lid on her feelings for him. To stop them from evolving even further. Because she had been starting to love this man.

That was the only explanation for how she could be hurting so much right now.

"I'm listening." He studied her, but his gaze was shuttered, revealing nothing of his own feelings.

Making her realize how much he'd let her in over the last weeks. How much he'd shared with her. It made losing that emotional intimacy hurt even more.

But there was no going back now. No ignoring this question that she kept returning to about him.

"When we spoke about your ex-wife," she began, twisting a cloth napkin in her lap, the linen hopelessly crumpled, "you said she didn't want children." The question was highly personal, and no doubt it revealed too much about what she felt for him. But it burned in her throat and she had to ask. "Did that mean—you didn't want children either?"

His mouth flattened into a thin line. An answer all its own even before he spoke.

"I hadn't given it much thought before Raelynn. And when she told me her wishes before the wedding…it wasn't a deal breaker for me."

She nodded awkwardly, her whole body feeling clumsy and strange. Maybe it was just because she didn't know where to put the hurt she was feeling. For her. For him. For those stupid romantic hopes that weren't ever going to amount to anything.

Because even if they were just in the early stages of a relationship, she couldn't spend her time with someone who didn't have the same kind of dreams she did for a future that would always include kids.

"I see." She stood from the table, needing to escape the table. The man. "I'll put Teddy down for his nap now."

"Lydia." James said her name with a tenderness she couldn't bear, but he didn't reach for her. Didn't touch her. "I think we should talk about this more."

"I can't." She'd been so judgmental of her mother

and her sister. But their foolishness couldn't compare to hers. "I'm—sorry."

She had built her life around children. Her family. Her job. Her future. Of course she had fallen for a man who didn't want them, at least not in the way she did. There was a kind of cosmic humor in it. Maybe she'd even laugh about it one day. Fifty years from now.

She fumbled with the safety belt on the high chair, her fingers not quite working. Or maybe it was because her vision was slightly blurred from tears she wouldn't let James see.

"Lydia, please." James pushed back his chair and came to help her. "I can put him down for his nap."

Ideally, she would have been able to be a professional. To still do the job she shouldn't have taken in the first place.

But right now, she couldn't even manage that.

"Thank you," she managed, before she retreated with as much dignity as possible.

She needed the quiet of her room for a few hours. To regroup. To figure out a way out of this impossible situation that wouldn't leave Teddy without a caregiver.

But one thing was certain. Now that she understood how wrong she'd been about James and the feelings she thought they shared, she couldn't possibly remain under the same roof even one more night.

Twelve

Three days before the new year, James sat in his office at the Texas Cattleman's Club and wondered if he should call Lydia. The days after their conversation had been painful, and he felt like they still didn't have any resolution yet on where things were headed between them.

Was she really ready to call it quits between them without delving deeper into what was upsetting for her? He understood why she was upset about the plans he'd made for Teddy without telling her. Because he had a different sort of life mapped out from the one she had planned for herself. Did that mean they couldn't compromise?

He feared the answer was yes. But that didn't mean they couldn't talk about it to be sure.

James hadn't wanted Lydia to leave when Teddy was clearly so attached to her, so he'd offered to work out of his office at the Texas Cattleman's Club for a few days. He had plenty to do with preparations for the New Year's Eve Ball, and the rest of the staff came in so sporadically between the holidays that no one noticed he was sleeping on his office couch.

Or, more accurately, *trying* to sleep on the office couch. Night after night, he couldn't stop dreaming about Lydia, and then he'd wake up feeling empty and alone, remembering the hurt in her eyes when he'd told her about the Masons.

Now, with the day of the ball closing in, he wondered if she even planned to follow through on their date. Checking the antique clock on the wall, he realized it was a quarter after nine. Past Teddy's bedtime, but not past Lydia's. Pulling in a deep breath, he punched the number for her cell into his phone. Waited while it rang once.

Twice.

"Hello?" Her voice sounded wary.

Even so, he was damned glad to hear it. He'd missed the sound of her, along with so many other things. Her scent. Her touch. The sweet way she cared for his nephew.

"Lydia." He hadn't thought beyond getting in

touch with her. Hadn't planned for how to wade through the awkwardness. "How are things at home?"

"Good," she answered quickly. "Fine. We're both—fine."

Right.

"I will need to meet Teddy's grandparents at the house midafternoon on New Year's Eve to welcome them. I wanted some time to speak with them and review Teddy's schedule."

"Of course. It's your home." Her words were clipped, her tone distant in a way that made him think of how her joy in the past had moved him. He felt the loss all the more deeply. "And I understood from our last conversation that I'm only here until your new arrangements are in place."

He ground his teeth, unwilling to tackle a complex conversation over the phone. Especially not when she was clearly still unhappy with him.

"I had hoped we could discuss that at the New Year's Eve Ball." He had been drawn to her practicality and sense of honor from their first meeting. He'd been banking on those qualities in her to ensure she showed up for their date. "Assuming you still plan to attend with me?"

She hesitated for a moment. "Do you really think it's wise for us to spend that time together when it's become obvious that…" She cleared her throat. Began again. "When it's clear now that our hopes for the future are so far apart?"

He thought it wise to at least have a discussion about what they wanted instead of assuming the worst about each other. But he clamped his tongue on that response. Besides, he wanted to be with Lydia. Being without her this week had made him realize how just how deep his feelings ran for her.

He loved her. But was he ready to risk his heart again on another woman who wasn't in it for the long haul? Regardless of the answer to that, he couldn't share how he felt about her. Not over the phone.

"I need a date for this event." He spelled it out in the only way he thought might convince her to attend. "And you could use an introduction to people who need your child care services. So the plan is practical, if nothing else."

"I recently learned there's such a thing as being too practical for your own good," she said drily. "But since I'll be unemployed again very shortly, I can't afford to turn down a good opportunity for my business. I will attend the ball with you as planned, James."

A possibility he hadn't considered hit him, something he should have thought of for Teddy's sake. What if she planned to quit even if the Masons didn't decide to take in their grandson? But he wasn't going to push for any more during an already difficult conversation. Hopefully he wouldn't need the answer to that at all. He confirmed the time for their date before he disconnected the call.

And wondered how on earth he could win back a woman hell-bent on ending things between them.

New Year's Eve was packed with Cinderella potential.

The Texas Cattleman's Club had been transformed into a shimmering silver-and-white haven. Long chains of white gladiolas were strung from the rafters, the delicate petals rimmed with hints of metallic glitter that made them shine in the candlelight. Tall candelabra draped with silver tulle and white ribbons stood atop every table in the room. A twelve-piece orchestra played along the back of the dining area, filling the room with lilting waltzes.

Lydia had splurged on a new dress for the event. Formfitting down to a little kick hem around her knees, the gown was pale green silk organza. Pairing it with an older pair of silver strappy heels, she felt as glamorous as she possibly could. Which wasn't to say she was the most beautiful woman in the room. But she looked like she belonged for at least one night. It hurt to think she'd never be a real part of this community that meant so much to James. Tomorrow, she'd return to her old life.

Alone.

Beside her, James Harris was the man everyone wanted to speak to, his job as esteemed president of the club underscoring how well liked he was. How respected. He was genuine and charming with everyone who greeted him. But despite the fairy-tale trappings of the evening all around her, Lydia had no illusions about how the night would end.

When midnight chimed, she wasn't just going back to her old life on the other side of town. She was also losing the man she'd fallen in love with, the sweet child she'd come to adore and all her illusions about herself.

She could never return to the old Lydia who used to feel good about her smart choices, her practical approach to relationships and her professionalism. Now she had to at least admit that love could rock anyone's world, skewing their perspective and making them behave in a way they normally wouldn't. She wasn't any less susceptible to that than any other woman. While she wouldn't ever get so swept away by love that she'd forget to supervise a child the way her mother had, Lydia also realized she'd been deluding herself into thinking she wasn't vulnerable to making other mistakes.

"Would you like to dance?" James bent closer to ask after he finished up a lengthy talk about yearling prospects with another rancher.

She couldn't help the shiver that tripped down her spine as he spoke close to her ear. The attraction that had been so apparent between them from day one hadn't magically faded when she'd discovered he had no intention of keeping his nephew.

"Yes. Thank you." She nodded, knowing everything she said to him sounded stilted. But she feared if she didn't carefully monitor her words, she would say something far too revealing.

So for now, she let him lead her to the dance floor and sweep her into his strong arms. His tuxedo was custom tailored, the black wool gabardine tapering to his narrow waist. There was a hint of sheen in the lapels of the jacket on either side of the crisp white pleats of his shirt. She wondered how he could appear equally at home in a Stetson and jeans as much as Hugo Boss, but some people simply seemed extraordinarily comfortable in their own skin.

"I've been wondering what you thought of the Masons," he asked as he spun her out of an easy turn, her silk organza gown flaring slightly.

As if she hadn't already been reminding herself that she was no Cinderella, the topic of conversation gave her another dose of cold reality.

Teddy's grandparents had been younger than Lydia imagined. They'd been in their early fifties, but could have passed for a decade younger. Physically fit and well dressed, they had been polite and kind. And yet…she couldn't shake the feeling that they were all wrong to raise Teddy.

"It matters more what you think," she reminded him, making the mistake of looking into his eyes. Holding his gaze made her think of more intimate moments with him. Of the ways he'd touched and kissed her. "I may be biased since I pictured something different for Teddy."

His brows pulled together. "I wish they would have responded to me sooner when I invited them to meet their grandson in the first place." He shook his head, a hint of frustration in his voice. "I realize their relationship with their daughter had been strained after she married Parker, but wouldn't you think that would be all the more reason for them to be eager to meet Teddy?"

"Yes." She couldn't stand the idea of that little boy enduring any more upheaval in his young life. "Unequivocally, yes."

"But in their defense, everyone processes grief in their own way. They might have needed that time to mourn before they came here." His grip shifted on her waist, his palm absently stroking for the briefest moment until he seemed to catch himself and still the movement.

"Perhaps." She couldn't say anything more, her senses too overloaded by that touch. By all that she would miss when she walked away from him.

She'd probably been foolish to show up tonight, to follow through with this doomed date. But she really did need the networking opportunity that it offered. Especially since she would be without a job soon.

"The comb is pretty in your hair," he said in a low, husky tone as the dance came to an end. "I'm glad you wore it tonight."

The crowd applauded for the orchestra as they took a break in their set. Lydia clapped, too, though her chest ached at the memory of James giving her the hair comb. Of how special Christmas Eve had been when they were together just one week ago. Or the long, breathless night she'd spent in his arms afterward.

Before she could respond, the microphone in front of the orchestra rang with a harsh sound. Turning, she spotted a dashing older man at the podium. He had a full head of white hair and piercing blue eyes, his skin deeply tanned. He tugged the microphone out of its stand so he could hold it in one hand, then he strode out from behind to podium to speak. The crowd quieted to listen.

James bent closer to whisper to her, "That's Gus Slade. He's a past president of the Texas Cattleman's Club."

She recognized the rancher from around town, the feud between the Slades and the Clayton family one of the bits of Royal history she'd picked up through local gossip. She welcomed the distraction for a moment to gather her defenses against leaning into the temping man beside her.

"Sorry for the feedback, folks." Gus Slade spoke into the microphone as he strode into the center of the raised platform near the orchestra. "We'll get back to the music in a minute. But first, I hope you'll indulge me. I have an announcement to make, and I want you all to be my witnesses."

The crowd settled into an even deeper silence. They all seemed to collectively hold their breath. Lydia peered over at James to see if his face gave any indication he knew what was about to happen since he'd helped put together the event. James must have felt her gaze since he glanced her way and shrugged.

"The new year is a time for a fresh start," Gus said, his voice strong and certain. "And more than anything, I want a chance to begin again, with the woman I love at my side." He paused for a moment, before someone turned a house spotlight on. The white-and-blue light fell around Rose Clayton seated at a table in the back. "Rose, would you do me the honor of becoming my wife?"

Rose and Gus?

The rest of the crowd seemed as stunned as Lydia felt, a shocked murmur reverberating through the well-heeled guests while Rose covered her surprised gasp with one hand, her eyes getting teary before she nodded quickly.

"Yes!" she called out across the room, standing up in her sparkly silver dress. "I will marry you, Gus Slade."

The microphone shrieked as Gus dropped it, forgotten, on the platform. He charged toward Rose with his arms open. The crowd clapped and there were a few cheers, although everyone still seemed taken aback by the proposal.

Behind her, Lydia heard a man say, "But I thought they were sworn enemies?"

Moved by the romantic gesture, Lydia felt her heart in her throat. The orchestra played a refrain from a popular country love song while someone turned off the microphone and the party got back under way. James guided Lydia from the dance floor, the romantic moment reminding her of all that was missing in their relationship.

It took her a moment to realize that she was following James out of the building into the garden, her thoughts still on the couple inside and all the love shining in their eyes. The night air was warm for December, but still a refreshing break from the crowded party rooms. It was quiet out here, where a few landscape lights gave the bushes and ornamental trees a silvery glow. More white lights outlined the walkways of smooth, decorative stone.

Here, there wouldn't be any networking opportunities for her child care business. Under the moonlight with James, there was only the two of them. Why would he bring her out here? And more important, how would she hold strong against his powerful allure?

He turned to her, his expression serious. "Seeing Gus and Rose in there made me all the more determined to speak to you about what's happening between us, Lydia."

"There's nothing else to say," she reminded him, unwilling to hurt any more than she already did. It would already be tough enough living in the same town with him. "I can't be with someone who doesn't want to have children in his life."

"But it's not that I don't ever want them," he clarified. "I'm just not ready right now. Today."

A whisper of hope swirled through her. And just as quickly, she tamped it down.

"I understand that's the right decision for you." She wondered what had made him so certain he wasn't ready to welcome a child into his life. "But in the meantime, a confused little boy who already lost one father is going to lose another man he's grown attached to."

"A child deserves to have a family in place. A family that's going to stay together." He spoke with passionate conviction. "The Masons have that, Lydia. I don't."

"You have me." She had thought that meant something to him.

"And look at how ready you are to walk out at the first sign of trouble." He shoved his hands in his pockets, his shoulders tense. "As soon as I brought up the idea of bringing the Masons to town, you shut down the discussion."

Surprise stole any response she might have made. Is that how he saw it? Perhaps she hadn't understood how deeply wary his failed marriage had made him. For that matter, maybe he hadn't known how incredibly gun-shy her past made her either.

"I'm sorry, James." She didn't know what else to say. The knowledge that he was hurting, too, didn't make the breakup any easier. If anything, it only increased the ache in her chest. She hadn't wanted things to end this way.

The vibration of a cell phone cut through the awkward silence, the soft hum emanating from James's breast pocket.

"I'd better see if it's the Masons," he muttered, reaching into his jacket. Stabbing at the screen. "Hello?"

He must have hit the speakerphone button because Samantha Mason's panicked voice cut through the quiet.

"Teddy's having an allergic reaction," the woman sobbed in a rush of words. "We're on the way to Royal Memorial Hospital, James. Please hurry."

Thirteen

James wasn't surprised when Lydia insisted on riding with him to the hospital. She might be done with him, but her attachment to Teddy was undeniable. Whatever her reason to be in the passenger seat with him, and then rushing into the emergency room with him fifteen minutes later, James was grateful as hell to have her at his side.

"I told them where the EpiPen was." James knew he'd said it more than once on the way to the hospital.

But the thought kept circling around in his brain after he'd hung up from Samantha Mason's frantic first call.

"You did. You showed it to them," Lydia reminded him again as they wound through the triage area to the desk. "Maybe the shot didn't help. Maybe they weren't able to give it to him fast enough."

He hadn't asked what happened when he got the call. He'd been too shaken up, too terrified. What if something happened to his brother's son, when protecting Teddy had been the only thing Parker had asked of him?

"We're here for Teddy Harris." He willed the nurse at the counter to give him good news. Tell him his nephew was okay. "I'm his legal guardian."

"He's in room three." She pointed to a door behind the nurse's station. "The doctor is in with him now."

James was already moving. Lydia's high heels tapped a quick beat to his longer strides and he slowed a fraction to give her his arm. His movements felt wooden, his body on autopilot.

She accepted his help in silence, her expression mirroring the fear that chilled his insides.

"He's going to be okay." He told himself as much as her. Needing it to be true.

The hospital room was quiet, after all. Surely there would be all sorts of noise and staff in motion if the worst was happening.

Still, dread filled him as he pushed the door open. Teddy's grandparents stood on either side of the toddler. Between them, Teddy lay in a hospital crib. Around him, monitors beeped quietly and an IV bag hung by the bed, giving some kind of fluids into the boy's tiny arm. An oxygen mask covered the lower half of his face. His eyes were closed, but James wasn't sure if that was because he was sleeping or because of the swelling around his eyes.

His skin was pink and splotchy.

James didn't know how he remained standing upright. But he thought it helped that Lydia squeezed his arm hard for a moment before she hurried to the baby's side. Her hands fell to his little knee through the white blanket that partially covered him.

"Is he—" James felt his throat close up tight.

Death had stolen everyone from him. *Everyone.* He could not lose Teddy.

His eyes burned.

"He'll be fine, Mr. Harris." A shorter man in a white lab coat stepped between James and the crib, offering his hand. "I'm Dr. Voss."

"He's okay?" James shook the man's hand, though half his attention was still on the other side of the room where Lydia leaned over the crib wall to stroke Teddy's dark curls.

A swell of love for her filled his chest, easing some of the fear. He turned back to the doctor, needing the rest of the story before he could believe Teddy would make a full recovery.

"He's stable now. The EMT crew faced the worst of it on the way over here." Behind Dr. Voss, Mrs. Mason released a quiet sob, a ball of tissues wadded up in one hand.

Teddy's grandfather moved around to the other side of the bed to be by his wife, sliding an arm around her shoulders.

The doctor continued, "We're still giving him some cortisone and antihistamines intravenously, and we wanted to keep him on supplemental oxygen for a little while. But we're monitoring him carefully just in case he exhibits any more signs of distress."

"What about his face?" Lydia asked from the bedside. "He's so swollen."

"We'll get some ice on that," the doctor assured her, backing toward the door. "I'll ask a nurse to come in and remove the oxygen in about thirty minutes, and we'll start some ice for the swelling. But it should go down on its own in time."

"He already looks better than—" Teddy's grandfather, George, interjected "—before."

"Don't be too hard on yourselves, folks." The doctor paused with the door half open. "You did the right thing coming in. Even if you had administered his EpiPen, we would have wanted to see him after that kind of a reaction."

Samantha Mason let out another sob behind her tissue as she sat down.

Relief flooded through James. "He's going to be okay."

"James, I'm so sorry." Samantha straightened from where she'd been slumped in a metal chair near the bed. "George had a snack pack of cereal that he eats sometimes when his sugar is low. We'd never give Teddy anything like that after what you said about the nut allergy, but we think he must have eaten a piece that fell on the floor. Right?" She turned to her husband for confirmation.

George shrugged. "I don't remember dropping any, but maybe I did. I was feeling a little shaky. But the next thing we knew, Teddy was wheezing."

James understood mistakes happened. It could have been him who'd dropped a piece of food that Teddy ate. Or Lydia. Still, he couldn't help a spike of frustration. "So what happened with the EpiPen?"

The couple exchanged looks before George answered, "When you showed it to us, I thought you took it from the top kitchen drawer in the island."

James shook his head. "I keep it in the diaper bag."

He knew the bag had been sitting on top of the island when he'd shown it to them. But it didn't matter now. He'd make sure the hospital sent them home with another. While he spoke with the Masons, Lydia rose and let herself out of the room.

His gaze followed her. Was she leaving for good? Or just getting a nurse? Maybe she simply didn't want to hear all the ways the Masons had endangered

Teddy. Truth was, he found it tough to hear the story, too. Especially since their babysitting had ended with Teddy in an oxygen mask, hooked up to an IV.

Guilt swamped him. He should've done so much better by his brother's child. Teddy was the only family James had left, and he hadn't taken that responsibility seriously enough.

Was this some kind of cosmic payback for almost giving up custody of the boy? He'd been a fool to ever consider it.

Samantha shivered, rubbing her arms as tears welled in her eyes again. "I was pulling out all the drawers in the island. I just kept thinking how we'd already lost Mandy, and now we were going to lose her little boy, too."

"I called 911 right away," George offered, shaking his balding head. "It all happened so fast."

James had heard enough. He really wanted to be with his nephew. "Anyone would have been scared to see that happen," he reassured them since there was nothing to be gained in arguing with them. "You must be exhausted after going through that. If you want to go back to the hotel, I can call you if there's any change in his condition."

He also really hoped Lydia hadn't left. But Samantha Mason was still visibly upset as she continued telling him about her daughter, Parker's wife. Between tears, she said, "And we never did see Mandy again. Never had a chance to heal our differences. Little Teddy is all we have left of our beautiful daughter now."

Something about the way she'd phrased it made James uncomfortable. Did they really see Teddy as a replacement for their dead daughter? James tried to offer some comforting words if only to speed the Masons out the door.

Teddy wasn't a replacement for anyone. He was an innocent boy who'd lost too much in his young life, and he deserved the best that James had to offer.

From now on, he needed to focus on his family.

That meant Teddy. He saw that all too clearly now. Teddy was his, now and always.

And, if he could find her, he wanted to tell Lydia that he finally understood what she'd been trying to tell him all along. That Teddy was his family. But the part that Lydia hadn't figured out yet was that she was his family, too. Because he was ready to claim Teddy as his son, and he wanted Lydia to be at his side when he did.

Lydia couldn't sleep when she got back to the house.

She put the kitchen back in order so Mrs. Davis wouldn't return from her New Year's holiday to find spoons and papers on the tile floor, but after that she went upstairs to pack her things.

Seeing Teddy in the hospital bed had been devastating. Rationally, she knew his exposure to tree
nuts could have happened to any babysitter. Yet
it upset her to think the Masons not only let the
substance into the house where their grandson had
a serious allergy, but then they hadn't even been
able to locate the medicine that could have slowed
the reaction and possibly prevented anaphylaxis.
Every second would have counted for that first
responder team when they arrived on the scene.

They could have lost Teddy.

Although as much as she'd grown to love the
little boy and his uncle, Lydia knew she had no
claim on them. They weren't hers to love. So she
had phoned her sister in the predawn hours, asking Gail to act as a babysitter if Teddy needed one
when James returned from the hospital with him.

Gail might be financially irresponsible, but Lydia
trusted her to watch a child. Even a severely allergic
child. That certainty in her gut made Lydia realize
she needed to make peace with Gail. Because they
were still family, and Gail had never asked her to
cover for her with the bachelor auction bid.

Lydia had involved herself in that situation on
her own. She was a caretaker. A fixer. And she
could tell herself that it was okay to say no to unnecessary crazy as many times as she wanted, but
she kept jumping in to help. She'd realized in this

last painful week without James that she needed to take ownership of her own life.

She had changed for the better because of knowing him. Lydia had a newfound acceptance of her family—and the pieces of herself that had been shaped by them. She would have to appreciate those changes, since they would be all she had left of her time with James. She understood herself too well to try to accept the path he chose, a path without Teddy.

When she heard the low hum of a car engine outside, she hurried to the front door, expecting to see her sister. She twisted the knob, tugging the double panels open, and was shocked to find James's black sedan rolling to a stop in the driveway.

A lump rose to her throat. The tug of emotions in her belly was nothing new around him, but it hurt far more now that she couldn't act on those feelings. Now that she had to find a way to forget about him.

The thought twisted sharply inside her, reminding her that wouldn't ever happen.

James stepped from the driver's side door, his gaze locking on her. "I'm glad you're here."

Opening the rear door, he leaned into the vehicle to unfasten the restraint on the car seat.

Lydia moved closer, wanting to see Teddy even though she knew every moment she spent with him only made it harder to leave. She needed to know he was okay.

"My sister's coming over," she told James while he lifted the baby in his strong arms, his shoulders blocking her view of Teddy. She closed the door behind them, then heard another car turning into the driveway. "That might be her now, in fact."

She reminded herself it was for the best to turn over her nanny duties to Gail for however long James still needed help with Teddy. Lydia didn't want to be in the house when they packed his things to send him to Amarillo with the Masons.

"I know. I spoke to Lloyd a few minutes ago."

"Lloyd?" Lydia followed James as he strode toward the house, trying to peek around his shoulder to see Teddy's face.

She'd changed into jeans and a sweater, but James still wore his tuxedo from the New Year's Eve Ball. The bow tie hung around his neck, the top button of his shirt undone. He still looked too handsome for his own good.

Too handsome for hers, at least.

James paused on the front mat, glancing down at her. "The bachelor she fell head over heels for, remember?"

"Right." She found it hard to think about her sister's drama with too much of her own crowding her thoughts and breaking her heart. "Of course."

Glancing back at new vehicle in the driveway,

she realized it wasn't Gail's compact. There was a man in the driver's seat of an exotic-looking sports car, but from the passenger side, Gail gave Lydia a wave.

Confused, Lydia waved back, then hurried after James as he stepped inside the house.

"Lloyd wants to give me a check to cover your sister's bid. I told him it was not necessary, but he was so insistent, we agreed he'd donate the money to the Pancreatic Research Cancer Foundation."

"Really? That's amazing." She couldn't fully process that news and the implications it might have when she really just wanted to see Teddy's face first. Distracted by worries about the baby, she stepped closer to James again. "May I just see him? Is he really okay?"

"He's still a little groggy." James dipped his shoulder so Lydia could have a better view of the boy. "The doctor said to just let him rest for a few hours and the last of the swelling should dissipate by evening."

"Thank goodness." Relief rushed through her, so strong it made her weak in the knees. She couldn't resist a final, gentle squeeze of Teddy's arm. A stroke of his fluffy dark curls. "I'm so glad he's okay."

"Me, too." James's gaze held hers for a moment, making her aware of how close they stood.

Heat grazed her skin, the pull of attraction so

strong in spite of everything. Stepping away from him was downright painful.

"Hello!" Gail called through the front door, knocking gently before cracking it open a sliver. "Can we come in?"

"Please do." James invited them inside. Gail and a tall, blond-haired man with a square jaw and aviator sunglasses.

Gail had the same "in love" glow that Tessa Noble had when she'd stopped by with Ryan earlier in the month. Gail introduced Lydia to Lloyd while James excused himself to put Teddy in his crib.

"Nice to meet you," Lydia said automatically as she shook Lloyd's hand, although her eyes followed James's progress up the main staircase.

"You, too," Lloyd said, tugging off his shades. "And we're going to stay out of your hair. We're only here for babysitting duty." He grinned. "You get two for the price of one with us."

Lydia tried to smile, charmed in spite of herself by Gail's new boyfriend. But it was hard to make small talk when her heart ached.

Once Gail and Lloyd went to watch over Teddy, there was nothing to keep Lydia here. Her gaze fell on the suitcases she'd already packed and set near the front door.

"There's a playroom near the nursery," she told them, thinking of all the hours she'd spent there in the last weeks, delighting in Teddy's accomplishments as he lost himself in playtime and forgot to be the confused, fractious little boy she'd met that first day at the Texas Cattleman's Club. "It has a sitting area—"

"We'll be fine," Gail assured her while Lloyd tugged her toward the stairs by the hand. Behind him, she mouthed silently to Lydia, "He's so hot!"

If there'd been any doubt what she was saying, Gail fanned herself before she had to focus on the steps.

"But—" She had hoped to speak with her sister longer. At very least, to apologize for intruding in Gail's business when clearly she had addressed the situation herself.

The couple holding hands were too far up the stairs now, however. They passed James, who pointed out the door to the nursery and the playroom on his way down.

Toward her.

Her throat closed right up at the thought of saying goodbye to him.

"Lydia, wait." He'd taken the time to change into dark jeans and a long-sleeved white T-shirt. He tugged one of the ribbed cuffs higher on his forearm as he strode into the living area. "Can we talk?"

"I was just—" She pointed to her suitcases, not sure what else there was to say. "I called my sister to take over for me until the Masons—"

"There will be no Masons." He took her hands in his, surprising her with his touch as much as his words. She looked up into his light brown eyes flecked with gold, and, as always, warmth tripped down her spine at the mere sight of him.

Sunlight spilled over her shoulders through the big windows, the holiday decorations casting rainbow reflections around the room.

"I don't understand." Unless…a horrible thought occurred to her. "Did they decide not to take him because of what happened? Is he too much trouble?"

"No." He shook his head. "Nothing like that. They love Teddy and feel terrible about triggering the allergy."

She relaxed slightly as the maternal defensiveness eased. "Then what do you mean?"

He squeezed her hands tighter, his thumbs stroking the insides of her wrists. "I can't describe the fear I felt last night when we walked into that emergency room. Not just a fear that I'd messed up my brother's one wish for me that I keep his son safe." He hauled in a long breath. "I knew I'd be devastated to lose him, too. Because I love that child, and I'm not going to ever let him go."

"Oh, James, that's wonderful." She was thrilled for him. For Teddy. "You'll make such an amazing father."

She was overwhelmed with the urge to hug him,

so she did. Even though it hurt to feel so much love for him, to feel so close to him, and not be able to share in the future he painted.

Because even though it was almost everything she could have wished for, the picture he painted hadn't included her.

The reality of that brought her back to earth in a thud of awkwardness over how she'd thrown herself into his strong arms to hug him. She tried to ease back.

Only he kept on holding her tight, burying his head in her hair.

"Lydia. I've missed you so much," he spoke into her hair, the scruff on his jaw snagging the strands.

Her heart pounded harder. She hardly dared to hope…

"I'm—" She'd already told him how she felt. So she clamped down on the thought now as she pulled away. "I know Teddy will be so happy to grow up here. Where he belongs."

Her eyes stung a little. Happy tears, she told herself.

"You belong here, too, Lydia. With me." His voice hit that deep note that rumbled right through her, even though it was softly spoken.

"I—" Blinking, she tried to focus on what he was saying. She couldn't afford to misunderstand when she was already holding together the pieces of herself from the heartbreak of the past week. "I can't be his nanny anymore, though. Not when—"

"Not as a nanny." He drew her closer again, curling a finger under her chin to look into her eyes. "As my wife." He let the words sink in. Holding her gaze with his. Canting closer to speak softly against her cheek. "Marry me, Lydia Walker. I can't get through another day without you in my life. I love you too much."

Happiness stole her breath, filling her with a shiny new hope that made her feel lighter. So light she might float right away with it.

"Really?" She closed her eyes, swaying into him, needing to hear it again.

"Every day without you has been painful. But I knew it was wrong to ask you to come back when I wasn't sure about Teddy. I think I was still grieving for Parker. Still feeling like I'd never have enough to offer a child of my own." He cupped her face in both hands, his gaze steady, certain. "But I've got everything he needs, because I love him."

"That's true." She arched up to brush her mouth along his, knowing she could help the Harris males find happiness. But more than that, she was going to love them, too.

"And it felt so right when I figured that out." He kissed her eyelids. Her cheeks. "But then, it got even better when I realized that I might still be able to win you back. Because it's not a family without you."

"Consider me won." She wrapped her arms around his waist, fitting against him like she was made for him. "I love you, too, James."

His expression lit up at her words. "I don't have a ring yet." He stroked her shoulders and peered down at her. "And I'm not going to rob you of a special proposal—"

"I'm not worried about that." She wasn't the kind of woman who needed a splashy display. It was enough to have her "over the moon" love.

"I can't let Gus Slade outdo me in the romance department." He arched a teasing eyebrow at her. "I want to give you the fairy tale, Lydia. You deserve that."

"I just need you." She smoothed her hands over his chest, feeling all that delicious male strength. Feeling the steady beat of his heart. "Everything else is a bonus."

"It's a new year today." He kissed her lips. A slow, thorough kiss that promised so much more, a lifetime of more. "A new start. And I can't imagine a happier way to begin it than having the woman I love in my arms."

She wasn't ever going to get tired of hearing him say that. A shiver of pleasure tickled her neck. Anticipation hummed through her.

She stepped away from him so she could lace her fingers in his. Leading him toward the staircase.

"Actually, I can think of one way that might add to our happiness." She felt breathless with new love. New hope. And a whole lot of desire. "Especially since we have babysitting help."

"I've heard that new parents need to make the most of their alone time." He caught her up in his arms, kissing her again until they were both breathless.

They stared at each other for a heated moment before their feet were moving again. Up the stairs, straight for the master suite.

Sometimes, no other words were needed.

Epilogue

Four weeks later

Rose Clayton Slade could have danced all night.

She and Gus had invited half of Royal to the wedding ceremony and reception held in one of the restored barns at the Silver C. They'd brought in patio heaters and obtained special permission from the local fire commissioner so they could celebrate their night in a place close to their hearts. She twirled under her groom's arm as he spun her in a country waltz they both knew all too well. Gus had hummed the same tune to her many, many years ago when he'd asked her to dance with him in this very barn.

She'd never forgotten the steps. And she wanted to repeat them with him a thousand more times at least.

When the music shifted to a more upbeat piece, Rose relinquished her new husband to one of his daughter's friends who wanted to claim a dance.

"I want a two-step when I come back," Rose whispered in Gus's ear before he kissed her on the cheek.

"I want that and a whole lot more," he told her with a wink.

How was it he could make her feel like a girl again, all blushing and flirtatious, when they'd argued like cats and dogs for so many years? Rose tried not to question it. She wanted to just be. To let this beautiful wedding reception unfurl all around her like an endless summer day. They'd paid the fiddler and his band to play as long as there were guests still in the barn, since all their friends from the Texas Cattleman's Club came out in force to celebrate.

It did her heart good to see all the couples together having fun, even outside the barn in the cooler night air where you could still hear the music. They'd put up a canopy strung with white lights, decked with more greenery and patio heaters. She was surprised so many people had made use of it in the cool evening. But James Harris and his new fiancée, Lydia, were so wrapped up in each other as she strode past them, she was sure they didn't even hear her say hello.

Which was the lovely thing about a wedding. Everyone could celebrate their love. If only her grandson had that in his life.

Ducking behind a rose-covered archway they walked through earlier, Rose breathed deep and looked up at the moon, savoring a peaceful moment alone before she went back inside. She was about to return to the barn when a familiar voice on the other side of the flower-covered arch stopped her.

It sounded like Gus's granddaughter, Alexis, was speaking in hushed tones to someone.

"No, I'm not worried," the woman was saying. "I'm pregnant, not helpless! I'll manage. It will be fine."

Rose nearly fell over straining to hear more, but the voice outside must have moved farther away. Not even remotely concerned about eavesdropping, Rose rushed outside to see if it really had been Alexis.

Pregnant?

It couldn't possibly be.

Except there, walking fast toward the front lawn of the main house, she caught a glimpse of Alexis Slade clutching a cell phone to her ear. Her back was to Rose, but the pink floral lace dress was unmistakable in the outdoor lights.

Rose felt faint.

She walked as fast as she dared in her tiered white wedding dress and turquoise-colored cowboy boots. She was not surprised to see her grandson, Daniel, charging toward Alexis, too, a look of determination on his chiseled features.

Not many women would have dared stop him with that look on his face. But those rules did not apply to grandmothers.

"Daniel." She double-timed her step to intercept him, tugging his arm.

His gaze stayed on Alexis for a long moment before he focused on her. "Yes?"

"Daniel, is it true?" She kept her voice low, mindful of guests even though they weren't close to anyone here by a stack of hay bales left out in case anyone needed an impromptu seat. "Is Alexis pregnant?"

His jaw jutted. "How did you find out?"

Her heart sank. She didn't need to ask if he was the father. She remembered seeing them together before. The spark between them was impossible to miss. Breaking them up had brought her and Gus together, and now Rose felt sick about it.

"Daniel, you have to—"

"I have." His dark brown eyes flashed fire. "I asked her to marry me, and she said it was too late. That I was only asking because of the baby."

"Were you?" She couldn't help but ask. But, seeing his expression and his patience worn thin, she changed tactics. "I'm sorry, Daniel. I—"

"Gran, you know I'd do anything for you. And I'm happy for you today. But I really need to go."

She nodded, seeing the way his shoulders bunched. His hands flexing into fists at his sides. She understood the way feelings could drive you to dark, unhappy places. She'd feuded with Gus for most of her adult life because she loved him and couldn't be with him.

It hurt to see him walk away. Not toward where Alexis had been, but toward his truck, parked close to the main house.

"Where's my bride?" Gus's voice called her from her worries.

She watched him stride toward her across the grass, so handsome and vital. A wave of love steadied her despite the ache in her chest.

"Sweetheart, what's wrong?" he asked as he came closer, pulling her into his arms. "You don't look like the happy bride who promised to meet me on the dance floor."

"I know." She nodded, gripping his hand. Needing his strength. "I just overheard that Alexis is pregnant."

Gus lifted a weathered hand to his face, covering whatever he might have said. She could see the shock in his eyes.

"The baby is Daniel's," she continued, wishing

she'd found a gentler way to break the news to him. She leaned into him, wrapping her arms around his waist. "I asked him about it, and he said he asked her to marry him, but she won't because he's only proposing for the baby's sake."

Gus stroked her back, hugging her closer. Until that moment, she hadn't realized how chilled she'd grown outside. She was shivering.

"What a mess we made," Gus said gruffly, tucking her against him.

"It was hard enough seeing them so unhappy. And now this?" She heard the music pause inside and she worried it might be time to cut the cake. "Gus, we need to go back. But promise me we'll figure out a way to get them together?"

She would gladly delay the honeymoon so they could put their heads together and figure something out.

Gus nodded. He took her hand and squeezed. "I've got an idea. So don't you worry about it for even another instant, Rose. I'm going to fix things this time. For good."

And at the strength of the conviction in his voice, a strength she wished she'd trusted in decades ago, she believed him. She tucked her fingers into the crook of his arm and started walking back toward the barn where their guests, their community, their future waited.

* * * * *

*How will Rose and Gus fix the mistakes they've
made with Alexis and Daniel?*

Find out in Alexis and Daniel's story.
Lone Star Reunion *by Joss Wood!*
The final installment of the six-book
Texas Cattleman's Club: Bachelor Auction series.

*Will the scandal of the century lead to love
for these rich ranchers?*

Available February 2019!

Texas Cattleman's Club: Bachelor Auction

Runaway Temptation *by USA TODAY
bestselling author Maureen Child.*
Most Eligible Texan *by USA TODAY
bestselling author Jules Bennett.*
Million Dollar Baby *by USA TODAY
bestselling author Janice Maynard.*
His Until Midnight *by Reese Ryan.*
The Rancher's Bargain *by Joanne Rock.*
Lone Star Reunion *by Joss Wood.*

Get 4 FREE REWARDS!

We'll send you 2 FREE Books plus 2 FREE Mystery Gifts.

Harlequin® Desire books feature heroes who have it all: wealth, status, incredible good looks... everything but the right woman.

FREE
Value Over
$20

---

*Flynn Parker and Sabrina Douglas are best friends,
coworkers and temporary roommates. He's becoming
the hardened businessman he never wanted to be,
but her plans to run interference did not include an
accidental kiss that ignites the heat that's simmered
between them for years...*

Read on for a sneak peek of
Best Friends, Secret Lovers *by Jessica Lemmon,
part of her Bachelor Pact series!*

They'd never talked about how they were always overlapping
each other with dating other people.

It was an odd thing to notice.

Why had Sabrina noticed?

Sabrina Douglas was his best girl friend. Girl, space,
friend. But Flynn felt a definite stir in his gut.

For the first time in his life, sex wasn't off the table for
him and Sabrina.

Which meant he needed his head examined.

After the tasting, Sabrina chattered about her favorite
cheeses and how she couldn't believe they didn't serve wine
at the tour.

"What kind of establishment doesn't offer you wine with
cheese?" she exclaimed as they strolled down the boardwalk.
Which gave him a great view of her ass—another part of her
he'd noticed before, but not like he was noticing now.

Not helping matters was the fact that he didn't have to wonder what kind of underwear she wore beneath that tight denim. He knew.

They'd been friends and comfortable around each other for long enough that no amount of trying to forget would erase the image of her wearing a black thong that perfectly split those cheeks into two biteable orbs.

"What do you think?" She spun and faced him, the wind kicking her hair forward, a few strands sticking to her lip gloss. He reached her in two steps. Before he thought it through, he swept those strands away, ran his fingers down her cheek and tipped her chin, his head a riot of bad ideas.

With a deep swallow, he called up ironclad Parker willpower and stopped touching his best friend. "I think you're right."

His voice was as rough as gravel.

"You're distracted. Are you thinking about work?"

"Yes," he lied through his teeth.

"You're going to have to let it go at some point. Give in to the urge." She drew out the word *urge*, perfectly pursing her lips and leaning forward with a playful twinkle in her eyes that would tempt any mortal man to sin.

And since Flynn was nothing less than mortal, he palmed the back of her head and pressed his mouth to hers.

Don't miss what happens next!
Best Friends, Secret Lovers *by Jessica Lemmon,*
part of her Bachelor Pact series!

Available February 2019 wherever
Harlequin® Desire books and ebooks are sold.

www.Harlequin.com

  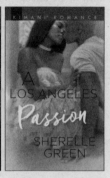
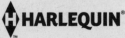